Summer of '63

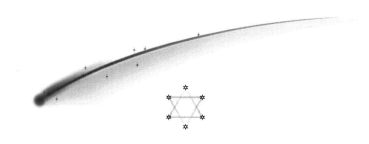

RODGER AIDMAN

Ann and Gayle,
Thanks for
everything.
Love,
Roddy 2012

Disclaimer

This is a work of fiction. All names and characters with the exception of a few well-known historical figures are products of the author's imagination and are not to be construed as real.

ACKNOWLEDGMENTS

"Surf City"
Words and Music by Brian Wilson and Jan Berry
©1963 (Renewed 1991) SCREEN GEMS-EMI MUSIC INC.
All Rights Reserved International Copyright Secured Used by Permission
Reprinted by permission of Hal Leonard Corporation

"Five Hundred Miles"
Words and Music by Hedy West
Copyright © 1961 by Atzal Music Inc.
Copyright Renewed
All Rights Administered by Unichappell Music Inc.
International Copyright Secured All Rights Reserved
Reprinted by permission of Hal Leonard Corporation

I wish to express my gratitude to my wife Susan for her love, support, encouragement and patience as I spent many hours at the computer writing this book.

Thank you to my son Andrew Aidman for his inspiration and love.

Special thanks to Steve Yagerman for his help with editing this book. His funny contributions helped me complete this project.

I wish to thank my nephew Tal Kitron for his assistance in obtaining permission to use lyrics of copyrighted songs in this book.

Thank you Shari Landa for your hard work proofreading this book.

Many friends and relatives have given me their support, love and inspiration. They have been a source of strength and wisdom in completing this publication.

Special thanks and love to: Ellyn Scanlan, Matthew Scanlan, Fran Conaway, Charles Conaway, Cindy Conaway, Carla Conaway, Frank Conaway, Carolyn Aidman, Amy Aidman, Evan Aidman, Rick Tarkington, Alice Tarkington, Suzannah Tarkington, Tim Tarkington, Ted Kloss, Susan Whitehouse, Tom Figlio, Marc Whitehouse, Sally Whitehouse, Ted Aidman, Nelson Cruz, Roger Cruz Sr., Oswald Cruz, Jonathan David, Mari-Luz Penaranda, Mac Cowden, Carl Hersh, Suzanne Crispell, Lilly Bottaro-Campbell, Bobbie Titman, Andrea Gutierrez, Lynn Katzen, Monica Cristobol, Maria Laurie, Phil Glatstein, Nick Riscigno, Fred Witkin, Allen Cox, Jan Sauvigne, Mark Saffer, Terri Aborlleile, Perry Casner, Lori Casner, Larry Suchman, Jerry Greenberg, Joyce

Beber, Barbara Phillips, Sara Orellana, Jean Soman, Bill Soman, Ed Sandor, Dave Zakus, Ellen Siegel, Stephen Colyer and Jill Reiter

Thanks to the helpful people at Createspace.

Cover art by Camille Arca.

Photographs of the author by Andrew Aidman.

This novel is dedicated to the memory of my parents, Jeanne and Sol Aidman.

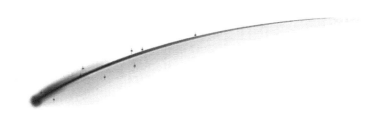

TABLE OF CONTENTS:

CHAPTER 1
BAR MITZVAH

THE RABBI'S STUDY at Temple Beth Ami was thick with cigar smoke. The shelves were lined with rows of books. Most of them were in Hebrew. Despite five years of Hebrew school, the ancient language of the Jewish people was still Greek to me. It was the last private study session with the rabbi before my bar mitzvah next Saturday. Rabbi Samuel May leaned in close to me, and I got a whiff of cheap cologne mingled with expensive cigar. We reviewed my Torah portion for the last time. His thick black mustache twitched slightly as he spoke.

"Our standard here, young man, is excellence. God smiles on the bar mitzvah boy who completes his haftarah with no mistakes. You have a lovely voice, and your chanting is on key, which is not the case with all bar mitzvah boys. If you work hard, you will make your parents proud this Saturday. You must work with diligence to achieve perfection."

"I'll do my best, Rabbi May. One problem: my voice. It's still changing. If it cracks during the service, all my friends will laugh at me, and I'll just die from embarrassment."

"Go over your speech a few more times, and you'll be fine. Don't worry, because you have prepared well."

The tip of the rabbi's cigar glowed red, and the white ash at the end of it grew longer. A cloud of exhaled cigar smoke expanded throughout the study as he continued to pontificate in his thick New York accent. He waved his arms in the air as if he were preaching to the entire congregation.

"The Torah was given to the Jewish people by God. It is the holiest of books, and it is a great sin if we treat the Torah with anything less than perfect love and respect." Clearing his throat and coughing, he continued, "I understand that in the old country, your great grandfather was a *sofer*. The scribe's job was to transcribe the Torah. Did you know that the writing of the Torah must be completed without error? Each of the 304,805 letters must be perfect. Some writing mistakes can be erased by scraping the ink off of the sheepskin parchment. However, if a mistake is made in writing one of the many names of God, no correction can be made. Because, young man, it is forbidden to erase the name of God. If an error is made, the sheet of parchment must be buried, and the Sofer must start over from the beginning of that section. The text is so holy that we are forbidden to even touch the writing on the parchment with our fingers. That is why I'm using this silver *yad* to point out our place as we chant." Staring straight into my eyes and arching his bushy eyebrows, the rabbi instructed me in his most commanding voice, "Perfection, Rodger. You must strive for perfection."

Rabbi May chewed on his cigar as he finished lecturing me on the sanctity of the holy scrolls. As he stood and turned to leave, the long gray column of cigar ash dropped from the end of his cigar. He didn't notice as it fell into the open prayer book.

✡ ✡ ✡

Saturday morning the synagogue was full, as my friends and family gathered to witness my bar mitzvah. I had a major case of *shpilkes*. It felt like a herd of cattle stampeding in my stomach. All eyes were on me as I sat in an honored place on the bimah. I was joined by the rabbi, the cantor, my father, and my grandfather.

The Saturday morning service began. My nervousness began to ease as the rabbi led the congregation in the familiar prayers that were repeated every Shabbos morning. Rabbi May motioned for me to come forward. I strode to the pulpit and led the congregation in the familiar and important Jewish prayer, the *Shema*.

"Shema yisroel Adonai eloheynu Adonoi echad.

Hear, Oh Israel the Lord our God the Lord is One."

Gazing out at the congregation, it seemed like most of the people I had invited to my bar mitzvah were smiling at me. I had asked Helen Christofilaki, a very cute gentile girl from English composition class, to come to the service. My crush on Helen was an open secret. She was sitting in one of the front rows and seemed to be watching me with admiration. We exchanged smiles. It was enjoyable being the center of attention. There was more than a little Jewish ham in me.

Confidently I took charge of the Sabbath service, leading the assembled crowd in traditional songs and responsive readings. The rabbi opened the Holy Ark and removed the Sefer Torah. It was time for me to chant my portion of the haftarah. With years of Hebrew school and Sunday school behind me, and having spent many hours studying and memorizing, a surge of confidence ran through me. This was my moment. The rabbi used the silver *yad* to help me keep my place. I sang out loud and clear. My haftarah was as familiar to me as a top-forty rock and roll tune.

My heart soared as I approached the end of my portion. My voice didn't crack as I sang from deep in my diaphragm. There were no stumbles or mistakes. In the front row my grandparents were beaming. They were proud that I had honored God and my Jewish heritage with a flawless performance.

As the service drew to a close, it was time for my speech. It was a brief talk and perhaps a little simple. I thanked my parents and grandparents for their love and support. I mentioned many of the aunts, uncles, and cousins who had traveled to Miami to attend my celebration. I expressed my regrets that my Texas cousins had not been able to attend. Both of my mother's older brothers, Will and Harry, had heart conditions and thought it best not to travel far from home.

A bar mitzvah tradition at Beth Ami was for the bar mitzvah boy to make a contribution to his favorite charity. For my *tzedakah*,

I would raise funds for the American Heart Association. High blood pressure and heart disease ran in our family, and my mother's youngest brother, Shuki, had died suddenly of a stroke last year at age 34. I concluded my speech with these words: "Let us pray that a cure for heart disease will soon be found. I thank all of you for honoring me by attending my bar mitzvah."

Rabbi May rose and approached me to offer his final blessing. I still could smell the odor of cigar smoke on his breath and emanating from his clothes. He placed his hands on my shoulders and prayed in full-throated Brooklynese. A funny thought suddenly flashed into my brain, and I had to put my hand over my mouth to suppress a laugh. Rabbi May looked and sounded like that crazy funny man Groucho. On the holiest day of my life, I felt like I was being blessed by Groucho Marx.

"God, and God of our fathers, bless this young man on this, the day of his bar mitzvah. Rodger, Rueven ben Sender, I encourage you to continue with your Jewish education. I hope you will join our confirmation class so that after three more years of study, I can bless you again on this pulpit. It is my prayer that someday you will stand under the *chupa* with a Jewish bride. May God bless you with many children and may you raise them in the tradition of our Jewish forefathers, believing in one God, the unifying God of our ancient religion."

After a brief pause to cough, he concluded my bar mitzvah service.

"May the light of the Lord illuminate you all the days of your life. Aw-mayne."

The congregation responded, "Aw-mayne."

✡ ✡ ✡

That evening a large crowd gathered at our house for my bar mitzvah reception. A tent was set up in the backyard and there were tables and chairs under it. My mother had worked for many days preparing the food that sat on steaming platters placed on long tables covered with white tablecloths. A wooden dance floor covered part of our large backyard. It was plywood, but it had a veneer that made it look like parquet. Our brand new RCA stereo record player was set up to provide music. There were long-playing records and some 45s with plastic spindle adapters stacked on the turntable. Stevie Bagelman, one of my best buddies, was serving as disc jockey.

Stevie had the best record collection of anyone I knew. His knowledge of rock and roll was amazing. Steve and I both thought that Beach Boys music was the best ever made. We were sure no one could ever top their awesome vocal harmonies. Most weekends Stevie came over to my house, and we jammed on our beat-up old guitars. Steve banged out the chords, and I picked out the leads. Our fantasy was to get great electric guitars and form our own rock and roll band. We'd be fighting off the girls for sure. I knew Stevie would keep the guests rockin' tonight.

"Noodleman, this is the best corned beef sandwich I've ever had," said my next door neighbor, Wood the Hood, mustard dripping from the corners of his mouth. "Your mom is a great cook. And those Swedish meatballs? I could eat a hundred of them. I'm going to the bar to get a glass of whiskey."

Whiskey? Maybe he thought the mustard-stained peach fuzz on his upper lip would allow him to pass as an adult.

"You Jews really know how to throw a party," he said, with only a touch of his usual sarcasm.

Most people considered Wood to be a juvenile delinquent. My sisters thought he was headed to Kendall, the dreaded youth detention center. Lately he had been bragging about stealing hubcaps and shoplifting from the Seven Eleven. I knew he was hanging out with older guys who liked to drag race late at night on the lonely roads out in the Everglades. Even though he was only thirteen, he claimed the older guys let him drive and race.

At school, even the toughest of punks would avoid fighting with the Woodman. His fights were not the usual pushing matches that occurred every afternoon after school. He really hurt the guys who messed with him. Me? I was a peaceful guy who stayed out of trouble. I was lucky that Wood the Hood had always been a good friend to me. At school and after school, he had served as my bodyguard on more than one occasion. My motto was, "If he's not hurting me, he's okay in my book."

"Time to get everyone dancing," said Stevie as he cued up Chubby Checker's new dance record "The Twist" on the turntable. As soon as the music started, Elizabeth, a distant relative, grabbed my arm and pulled me onto the dance floor. She's my fourth cousin twice removed or something. Whatever the connection, it wasn't far enough removed for me. To be honest, no one was really sure if we were related or not. Elizabeth was a tiny girl without an ounce of fat on her. She was also a showoff and totally boy crazy. When she was a baby she pronounced her name "Littlebit" and that's what her parents and brothers still called her. Everyone else called her by her other nickname, Bitsy.

Bitsy's grandparents and my mother's parents, Grandma and Grandpa Wise, had come to Ohio from Poland as teenagers, seeking religious freedom and safety from the pogroms. They arrived in the golden land together at Ellis Island, under the protective gaze of the Statue of Liberty. Because we were *landsmen*, our families gathered for holidays and celebrations. For as long as I could remember, at every family get-together, Bitsy would try to get me alone and kiss me. I was ready for a kiss, but not one from my hot-to-trot distant cousin. She was really being annoying.

Bitsy and I joined the couples and individuals twisting the night away. Nice thing about the Twist is you don't really need a partner, and you can pretend everybody is your partner. Little kids were twisting. My parents were twisting!

Bitsy kept pulling me close, and I kept backing away as we twisted high and low. Our hips moved round and round as Chubby Checker commanded. When the music stopped, she whispered in my ear, "Hey, bar mitzvah boy, you're a man now. Give me a little kiss, will ya, huh? I like you. I love you. Kissy kissy."

"Lay off, Bitsy. There are plenty of guys around for you to kiss. Bagelman is playing my favorite slow dance. Why don't you go help him pick out 45s? Better yet, go eat a cocktail wiener. I'm going to see if Helen Christofilaki wants to dance with me."

As the sweet strains of Brenda Lee's "All Alone Am I" played, I walked over to Helen. She seemed to sparkle and looked even prettier than she did at school. It was the first time I had seen her wearing lipstick and a little bit of makeup. Her usually straight black hair was beautifully wavy tonight.

"Hey, Helen, did you know this song was written by a Greek composer named Manos Hadjidakis?" A little unsure of myself, I stuttered , "Do ya…do ya…do ya… do you wanna dance?".

"Uh, why…yes. I'd love to dance with you, Rodger. A Greek wrote this song? Just like in school, you're always full of interesting information," replied the dark-haired, dark-eyed, fair-skinned Helen. She hesitated for a second and then smiled as I took her hand and led her out on the parquet.

I instinctively tried to pull Helen close for a romantic slow dance, but she gently pulled away and insisted that we dance in the formal slow-dance position. I had one hand on her hip and the other held her shoulder. The width of three Frisbees separated our bodies. She would not put her face next to mine and dance cheek to cheek. Respectfully and just a little frustrated, I held my hand very still on her hip. We started to dance. At the exact same instant we both moved forward and stepped on each other's toes. Awkward? To say the least.

My sisters had taught me how to dance many years ago. They told me that girls always like it when a boy is a strong leader on the dance floor. Feeling the music, I started to lead, and Helen gracefully followed. Brenda Lee crooned and cried about her heartbreak and loneliness. Helen and I glided across the parquet in time to the music and spun around, orbiting each other. Helen was dancing with me. We were a couple. I looked into her dark eyes and saw a glimpse of my own reflection. I looked like a happy man. When the music ended, I walked her slowly off the dance floor.

Smiling sweetly, Helen said, "Thank you for the dance. You won't believe it, but it's the first time I've ever danced with a boy.

In church they tell us that boys and girls dancing together is a sin. But I really wanted to dance with you today, Rodger, because it's the day you have become a man." She leaned close to me and whispered in my ear, "Don't you think Brenda Lee's voice is dreamy?"

I could feel a huge grin spreading across my face. Was this feeling love?

Stepping back from me, Helen continued, "Rodger, thank you for inviting me to your bar mitzvah. This morning was the first time I've been to a Jewish church. Your mastery of God's holy language is very impressive. Many of your Sabbath prayers are also found in our Christian prayer books. I hope someday you'll come to prayer group with me at my church. I'm sure you know that the Jews are God's chosen people. The survival of the Jewish people and the rebirth of the nation of Israel are proof that we are in the last days and that Jesus is returning soon to take all Christians to heaven."

A little disappointed at being preached to by this lovely girl, I wondered, "Does Helen like me and want to spend more time with me or is she just looking to save my soul? Why was I falling for a non-Jewish girl?" My parents would not approve.

"Hey, everybody! It's limbo time! Time to see who can limbo the lowest. Everyone out on the dance floor," DJ Stevie Bagelman sang out.

Almost all of the kids and a large number of the adults lined up to limbo under the limbo pole being held by my two older sisters. We all moved rhythmically to the strains of Chubby Checker's other big dance hit "Limbo Rock". Every dancer made it under the pole on the first pass. Each time the bar was lowered, a few fell as they bent backward trying to limbo under the pole. After several rounds there was only one person left standing—Bitsy. The girls lowered the limbo pole even closer to the ground, and the limber Bitsy bent way back, trying to limbo under it. Halfway under the pole, Bitsy lost her balance and fell backward. Her short skirt rode way up her legs, exposing her white panties. Not at all embarrassed, unlike every other girl I knew, she lay there laughing and kicking her legs around. After all the boys had a good look at her legs and underwear, Bitsy finally stood up and walked over to Stevie Bagelman and gave my astonished friend a quick peck on the cheek. Bagelman recovered his composure and started playing Jamaican singer Harry Belafonte's version of "Hava Nagila" from the *Belafonte at Carnegie Hall* album.

Everyone gathered in a circle, holding hands. I was pushed to the center while my friends and family danced the hora around me. The circle moved in and nearly crushed me. Friends and family embraced me with love. Several of my buddies from Hebrew school brought a chair to the center of the circle and pushed me down into it. They lifted me above their heads and carried me around like a conquering hero. I leaned back and almost immediately began to lose my balance. The chair tipped backward at a dangerous angle. Fear of a disastrous fall sent a chill up and down my spine. As the boys nearly dropped the chair with me in it, the men came to my rescue. Dad and his brothers, Uncle Ted and Uncle Sam, along with my Uncle Larry moved quickly and pushed the chair back upright. They held it firmly with their strong hands. With the chair upright again, my friends and loved ones danced me around and around, and lifted me high in the air. What a relief when the music ended, and the chair was lowered. I was back on terra firma.

"Roddy, come over here and sit down. I have something for you." Grandpa Noodleman downed a shot of whiskey and slammed the shot glass down on the table. "Ah. This schnapps is goot," he said in his slurred Yiddish accent.

Stevie Bagelman, Wood the Hood, and Clifford Glick, a guy from my Hebrew school class, sat down at the table with Grandpa and me.

"Roddy, you are a good boy. My papa, Teyve the Sofer, would have been proud of you this morning. You read your Torah portion without a mistake while wearing his tallis. My papa's prayer shawl is one of the only possessions I brought to America from Russia."

Grandpa reached into his pocket and pulled out his thick wallet. He extracted a wad of twenty-dollar bills from it. My friends watched wide-eyed as he slapped five twenties down on the table in front of me. Quickly and greedily I picked up the twenties and stuffed them into the secret pocket in the lining of my suit jacket.

"These are all Jewish boys?" Grandpa asked, as he poured himself another shot of whiskey.

"Sure, Grandpa." I lied because I didn't want him to know that Wood the Hood was not a Jew.

Grandpa handed each of my friends a crisp, new twenty-dollar bill saying, "Don't go out with *shiksas*, boys. Marry Jewish girls and have many, many good Jewish children."

"Wow. Twenty bucks. Sure, Gramps. I'll marry a Jew," said Wood, nodding his head enthusiastically. "Can you get me a shot of that schnapps, too?"

Grandpa got up and embraced me. "I left Russia at age fifteen and never saw my mama or papa gain. Now I'm celebrating my American grandson's bar mitzvah. I am a blessed man." He was starting to cry as he handed me five more twenty-dollar bills. Grandpa threw down another shot of whiskey and toasted me with a hardy "*L'chaim*". He rubbed the top of my head and said, "*A gezunt ahf dein kop*. Do you boys support Israel?"

"I love Israel, Gramps," said Wood the Hood. Glick and Bagelman nodded their heads enthusiastically.

Grandpa gave each of the boys another twenty-dollar bill, which they accepted with gratitude and utter amazement.

"Moishe, you're *shicker*," scolded Grandma as she discovered Grandpa emptying his wallet. She smacked him hard on the shoulder and snatched the wallet out of his hands. She pulled the remaining cash out and wrapped in it her handkerchief. Then she stuffed the handkerchief into the bodice of her dress. He protested in rapid Yiddish as Grandma Noodleman led him away by the hand. Grandpa staggered slightly and Grandma, all four-foot-six of her, supported him and guided him to the couch.

Across the room, Uncle Larry, a jewelry salesman who had driven down from Michigan, motioned for me to come over to him.

"Roddy, *mensch*, mazel tov. You're thirteen now, and I want to be the first to offer you a cigar." He pulled a fat stogie out of his coat pocket and bit the end off of it. He put the cigar in my mouth and lit it with his Zippo lighter. "Just puff on it a little bit. It's a Cuban. Smuggled, of course. A buddy of mine gave me a box of them. He's in cahoots with these mobsters from Chicago. They get cigars from their Cuban mobsters friends who live in Miami. Down in Havana, Castro took the mob's casinos away, and they'll do anything to get those money machines back," said my uncle, as he puffed and chewed on his cigar. "The mafia and the CIA have been trying to bump off that arrogant tin-pot dictator Fidel for years. They even tried poisoning his cigars. You can't believe the crooked stuff going on in this country."

I imitated my uncle puffing and chewing on the cigar for a few seconds. It tasted bitter in my mouth, and I started to cough on the smoke. My eyes started to water, and my stomach started doing the Stroll. Feeling queasy, I tried to put the cigar down in the ashtray but it fell, still smoking, to the floor.

"I don't think I'm ready to smoke 'em like you and Groucho," I choked.

"Don't worry. Keep smoking. You'll learn to like it. Part of being a man is liking things you never thought you would," laughed Uncle Larry.

The party continued late into the night. Couples slow danced, wrapped in each others' arms. Stevie Bagelman and Bitsy danced with their bodies pressed tightly together. She pulled his face toward her and kissed him passionately. He pulled her body into a wraparound embrace. They let their hands slide down each other's back. Bitsy kissed Stevie again, as he massaged her buns with both hands. He pushed her short skirt high up her legs. How far would they go? When the music stopped, Bitsy and Stevie floated hand in hand through the backyard gate and out of everyone's sight to the other side of the hedge. How far they went I could only imagine.

Guests approached me to say good night and again say "Mazel tov." Many handed me envelopes with cards and, I hoped, generous checks inside.

Helen came up to me and stuck out her hand. "My dad is here to pick me up. I want to thank you again for inviting me to your bar mitzvah. Congratulations. Or should I say 'muscle tough'? I had a wonderful time. See you Monday at school," she said, as she warmly shook my hand.

I watched Helen walk away and looked around at the remaining guests. Some were still dancing, and others were munching on the sweets my mother had baked. Over in the corner of the yard something moved behind the palm trees. It was Wood the Hood, standing by himself with his back to the party. I walked over to see what mischief he was up to. He had filched a bottle of Jack Daniels from the bar and was swigging it down.

"Great party and great booze," he burped. "Have a slug of this whiskey. It'll make you feel great." He burped again, grabbed his stomach, and then vomited violently against the back fence.

"Uh. Glad you could make it to the party. Have fun, Wood," I said to my heaving friend as I walked back into the house.

My younger sister, Amy, walked up to me and pointed across the room. "Hey, Roddy, check out Cliff Glick. Some of the older folks must think that he's you. He's been racking up envelopes meant for you and sticking them in his coat pocket."

I walked over to my Hebrew school classmate and said, "So glad you could drop over, Cliff. Just because we look a little bit alike doesn't mean you get to keep my bar mitzvah presents. Taking other people's money might get you in real trouble some day. Hand over the envelopes."

"Sorry, Rajah. I was going to bring them to you later. Pretty funny that those *alte cockers* were giving me your presents. You did a great job this morning, and it's been a fun party. It's amazing that your mom catered the whole party herself. I am stuffed to the gills. The guests have polished off most of the delicious food she made."

Taking the envelopes from Glick, I responded, "Next week it's your turn. Are you ready to be the bar mitzvah boy? Maybe at your reception someone will give me some of your presents."

"My party is going to be at the DuPont Plaza Hotel downtown. It will be in the rooftop restaurant with an incredible view of the lights of downtown Miami and Biscayne Bay. My parents are having it catered by the best kosher caterers in town. They hired a seven-piece dance band, too. Everyone's coming. You can bring your cousin Bitsy. I'd kind of like to get to know her much better."

"I'll bet you would. It looks to me like Bagelman will be bringing her. They were really going at it tonight," I laughed. "Hey, Glick, check your pockets again, will ya?"

Clifford reached into the secret pocket in his suit jacket. Sheepishly, he handed me two more envelopes.

"Sorry, Charlie. I must have missed a couple. So what are you going to do with all that bar mitzvah loot, Rodg?"

"Travel, man. Mom and Dad said I could take a trip to Texas to visit my relatives after school's out for summer. I'll stay with my teenage cousins, Suzy and Marilyn, who live in Dallas and couldn't come to my bar mitzvah. Another cousin, Mark, lives in the small town of Clarksville. He's thirteen, too. No bar mitzvah for him, though. His mom isn't Jewish, and they go to church. It's rumored that he rides a Brahma bull. I get to travel all by myself. Now that I'm officially a man, it's time to see the world."

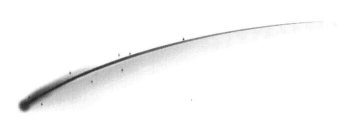

CHAPTER 2
EXODUS

ONLY THIRTEEN YEARS old and my parents were dropping me off for a two-day bus ride that would take me all the way to Texas. First, my teenage cousins Marilyn and Suzy would host me in Dallas. I only vaguely remember them. They had come to visit us in Akron, when I was three or four years old. There were black and white photographs in the family album of us playing together. Somewhere deep in my brain there were memories of being teased. Did Marilyn trap me on the up-side of the teeter-totter? Did she hold me down while I kicked and screamed, and Suzy painted my mouth with bright red lipstick? My parents wanted me to get to know my cousin Mark, who lived in the small, northeast Texas town of Clarksville. He had just finished eighth grade, too. I pictured him riding on his horse out on the range, with his six-shooter in his holster. My folks wanted me to experience small-town life, if even for only a few weeks.

I was hoping Texas was just like the cowboy movies I loved to watch. The adventure of a lifetime was just in front of me. This would be my first time away from home since we moved to Florida from up north. In 1959, when I was nine, my parents decided to uproot our family from Akron, Ohio, to live in Miami. The folks had decided that warm South Florida was a better place to raise their family than in the snow belt of northeastern Ohio. My mother's father, Grandpa Wise, was going to live with us in our new house in Miami. He had already sold his banyan tree shaded house in the section of

Miami called Coral Gate. Mom was hoping that living with his active, creative grandchildren would help Grandpa begin to enjoy life again. There had been no joy in Grandpa's life since his true love, Grandma, died of a stroke a year earlier. Like the ancient Hebrews led by Moses, the Noodlemans were making their own exodus, not to the land of milk and honey, but to a land of oranges and coconuts.

To save money, Dad decided to rent a truck from a new company called U-Haul instead of hiring a moving van company. The whole family worked together, and we moved the furniture from our house into that orange rectangle of a truck. It looked like there wasn't enough room in the U-Haul for our old upright player piano. Because I begged and begged, Dad nearly broke his back rearranging the furniture in our aluminum ark. Finally, we managed to squeeze that piano in. The U-Haul was so full that Dad was barely able to latch it shut.

Many tears were shed as we drove away from the only house we'd ever lived in. We waved goodbye to our playmates as we drove away from our familiar, tree-shaded West Hill neighborhood. As we drove past Portage Path School, a wave of sadness washed over me. It was like being pulled up by the roots in hopes of being replanted in the modern promised land.

A driver was hired to follow us in the U-Haul. He had an unpronounceable Polish name, chewed tobacco and seemed to spit constantly. It was impossible not to notice the brown stains on his teeth.

Mom and Dad piled their five kids into our green Olds 88. My nine-month-old baby brother, Evan, was placed in a car bed that sat on the floor of the backseat. Sitting up front between Mom and Dad, I was more comfortable than my three sisters, crowded in back with the baby at their feet. When he cried, we took turns holding him. Sitting up front, I felt special even though I could feel my sisters' jealous stares on the back of my head.

Thanks to President Eisenhower's road construction, we cruised on the brand new Ohio and Pennsylvania turnpikes. After several hours cruising along at 60 to 70 miles per hour, we exited the four-lane turnpike and started traveling on an old two-lane highway. The mountains of western Pennsylvania were steep and scary. Traffic came to a complete stop for almost an hour until we were finally waved past a jack-knifed semi that blocked most of the road. We started climbing a narrow winding mountain road. My sisters and I all felt our ears pop from the altitude at the same time. The strange feeling in our ears made us all bust out laughing.

Hoping to get many miles from our Ohio home, Dad drove on and on into the night. He started looking for a place for us to stop, as the kids got cranky from being cooped up in the car for so many hours. Finally, at 5:00 in the morning, on a lonesome country road in West Virginia, he found a motel with a vacancy. The motel was really an old farmhouse owned by an elderly couple. There were only two beds. The baby dropped his bottle as he fell asleep in the car seat placed on the floor. My little sister snuggled between Mom and Dad on one bed. I shared the other with my two older sisters. Exhausted, we collapsed and fell asleep in each other's arms just as dawn was breaking.

Back on the road the next afternoon the going was slow. There were only a few newly constructed segments of Interstate 95 open. We passed farms with large fields of corn, tomatoes, soybeans, and tobacco. Cows and horses grazed in the grass. There were goats, sheep and pigs in the farmyards. It took us two days to travel through the countrysides and towns of Virginia and North Carolina. Life in the rural South looked so different from the neighborhood that had sheltered me in Akron.

Getting restless from long hours squished together in the car, my sisters and I started teasing and poking each other. Mom and Dad finally lost patience with us. To get me away from my sisters they decided to let me ride in the U-Haul with the hired driver. I was fascinated by the huge chaw of tobacco he kept in his mouth. Every once in a while he would lean out the window and spit out tobacco juice, saying, "I just left my mark on another state. There's one for North Carolina."

We were listening to music on the radio in South Carolina when suddenly the program was interrupted to announce that a hurricane warning had been raised for the state of South Carolina. Hurricane Grace was bearing down on us. As the wind picked up, we pulled into a motel in Orangeburg, relieved to have found shelter.

No one slept that night, as we lay awake listening to the wind howl. It huffed and it puffed like the big, bad wolf. The lightning flashed continuously and the thunder was deafening. The doors and windows rattled and creaked but did not blow in.

The weather calmed at dawn as the storm moved inland. Power lines were down and the electricity was out. Dad pulled some downed branches off the Oldsmobile and then we all piled back into the car. We continued driving south, past fallen trees and road signs. I had never seen so much destruction. We were delayed where the road was blocked by tree trunks. Spontaneous crews of local men with axes, hatchets and chain saws cut away large enough segments of the trees for us to drive through. After a few delays, we were able to continue down the highway and out of South Carolina.

We continued on through hot and humid Georgia until we finally crossed the state line into Florida. Dad had been advised not take the newly constructed Florida Turnpike. He was afraid the U-Haul would not be able to travel at the minimum speed required on the new toll road. So we traveled slowly through every small coastal town on the Atlantic coast of Florida. Stopping at countless traffic signals on US-1 we probably averaged less than 30 miles per hour. It was thrilling each time we caught sight of the Atlantic Ocean. Dad took us out on A1A, and we drove passed Cape Canaveral, launch pad of astronauts. We all marveled at the sight of the tall launch pads visible on the horizon.

The United States was sprinting to catch up to Russia in the space race. President Kennedy promised we would land a man on the moon by the end of the sixties. Project Mercury was completed. The rockets and spacecraft for Projects Gemini and Apollo were being built. We had to beat the Russkies to the moon. If the communists landed on the moon first, we were afraid they would set up a military base there and defeat us in the cold war. The green and blue waves breaking and rolling out past the white sand dunes at Cocoa Beach beckoned seductively.

We finally made it to Miami in the middle of the night. Everyone was dead tired after driving nearly twenty-four hours straight from that last motel stop in South Carolina. Unfortunately the directions we had been given to our new home were incorrect. Instead of taking Southwest 87th Avenue, we turned onto Southwest 82nd Avenue. Dad made a turn on what he thought was Southwest 52nd Street, the location of our new home. In reality, we were still a mile east of the house Dad had bought. We made a left onto an unpaved road leading to a construction platform built for steam shovels digging deep into the swampland. The swamps of southwest Dade County were being converted into lakes.

Limestone and sand dug from rock pits were being used as a construction material for new homes. This newly dug rock pit was already named Lake Catalina and would soon be the sight of prestigious south Florida lakefront homes.

We followed the dirt road right into the middle of Lake Catalina. It was pitch dark and it looked like there might not be enough room to turn the truck around. The road was blocked by bulldozers and trucks loaded with sand and rock that had been dug from the swamp. The driver backed the truck dangerously close to the twenty-foot drop at the water's edge. The back tires started to slip on the loose sand and gravel. It looked like the truck and all our belongings were going to crash into the water. We all screamed for the driver to stop. At the last second, he slammed on the brakes and shifted into first gear. The wheels spun and spun. They finally grabbed on to some solid ground, averting a huge disaster. After much anger and confusion, the truck was turned around, and we escaped from the middle of the rock pit. Exhausted and completely worn out, we finally arrived at our new home in the suburbs of South Miami.

The move from Ohio to Florida was four years ago, and I hadn't been more than twenty miles from Miami since then. It was extremely exciting to be heading off on my own to spend the summer in Texas. Visions of cowboys and Indians and sheriffs keeping towns lawful with their six-shooters danced in my head.

C H A P T E R   3
CORAL GABLES BUS TERMINAL

W E PULLED UP to the Coral Gables bus terminal and immediately smelled the diesel exhaust coming from the buses huffing and chuffing like racehorses at the starting gate. It was finally time to leave on my long-awaited trip to Texas.

The bus terminal was an old Florida building constructed from large segments of coral rock. Each rock was full of tiny fossils from when the coral lay on the floor of the ocean millions of years ago. The local hub of a modern transportation system had been built from the ancient mineralized remains of the coral found offshore and under the thin topsoil of South Florida. Ancient stone blocks of coral made the bus station look almost like it had grown straight out of the ground. The blocks had been bleached white by the sun and were textured with lacy patterns of fossilized coral. It felt like fine sandpaper when you ran your hand over it.

I was fascinated by the coral reefs that grew in warm South Florida waters. The best day ever in eighth grade was a snorkeling trip to the Keys led by my very cool science teacher, Mr. McAroon. We took a school bus down to John Pennekamp Coral Reef State Park. The whole class spent the day diving on the reefs, which were a couple of miles offshore in warm, shallow water about a half-hour boat ride from Key Largo. The colorful schools of sergeant-majors and angelfish swimming above the reefs were unforgettably beautiful. The coral colonies were spread out over a large area. Coral are some of the most unique creatures on earth. We learned it is an animal that builds colonies that look like a rock but has lacy tentacles that look like a plant. Imagine a weird creature that can reproduce both sexually and asexually.

The bus station matched the architectural style of Coral Gables. There were also arches of coral rock at the entrances to the beautiful city designed by George E. Merrick and promoted by the perennially defeated presidential candidate William Jennings Bryan. It was easy to tell when you left the bland suburbs of Miami and entered the prosperous Gables.

During the development of the new Miami suburbs, most of the large trees had been bulldozed. Concrete block and stucco homes of similar designs had been built to accommodate the large number of people moving to Miami from up north in the '50s and '60s. The new Miami suburbs were laid out in uniform, square blocks that lacked character and interesting architecture. In contrast to the little boxes found in the new developments of Dade County, the homes in the Gables were unique in their styles and floor plans. The wide avenues of Coral Gables were shaded with large oak trees. In the summer, it always seemed several degrees cooler in the beautiful and shady Gables.

Mom and Dad walked me into the bookstore located in the bus station. My friends and I often browsed in the bookstore. The place had a forbidden feel to it, and I hoped to find something interesting to read on the trip. I found a paperback copy of Robert A. Heinlein's science fiction novel *Stranger in a Strange Land*. Several of my friends had read it and told me it was about a human raised on Mars who had telepathic powers. The main character came to Earth from Mars and started a new religion that had sex as one of its sacraments. We were all ready to convert. The plan was to start reading that novel right after I finished the last few chapters of *Exodus*, which I had smuggled from my parents' bookshelf. With forty-eight hours on the bus ahead of me, I was sure I'd have plenty of time for reading.

After perusing the racks of magazines, I picked up the latest *Mad* magazine, a *Superman* and a couple of *Archie* comics. I slipped them into my backpack along with some peanut M&Ms.

On the top row of one of the racks stood a row of forbidden magazines covered in brown paper. I gazed at them with curiosity. Everyone knew that *Playboy* was on sale at the bookstore. It was against the law to show the sexy cover of the magazine in public view. I felt guilty even looking at the brown paper covering the *Playboy* magazines. Some lucky friends at my junior high had seen the pictures of naked girls in *Playboy*, but I hadn't had the good fortune. Maybe someday I would turn the scandalous pages of a *Playboy*.

"Why don't you visit the bathroom before the long trip, Rod?" said my Dad.

There were four bathrooms at the Coral Gables bus terminal: "White Men", "White Women", "Colored Men" and "Colored Women". Segregated bathrooms. I wondered if they were separate but equal. I didn't have the nerve to go into the colored bathroom and see for myself. As I walked into the white men's bathroom, a Negro janitor carrying a mop and bucket walked out. He was allowed into our white bathroom to clean up after us. Why would anyone even care if a black man used a white toilet?

The announcement came over the loudspeaker. "Now leaving, express Greyhound to New Orleans with stops in Miami, North Miami, Fort Lauderdale, Pompano Beach, Boca Raton, Palm Beach, Stuart, Vero Beach, Lake Wales, Orlando, Deland, Gainesville, Lake City, Tallahassee, Pensacola, Mobile, Mississippi City, Gulfport, Biloxi, and New Orleans." Holy cow. If this was the "express", where did the milk run stop?

Before heading to the bus, I stopped for a drink at the water fountain. A sign above the fountain read "Cups for Colored". Had a Negro kid ever had the nerve to put his lips to the fountain reserved strictly for whites? "I'd rather drink from a cup, anyway," I thought, as I eyed the torn, yellowed paper cones that colored people were supposed to drink from. As I sipped from the "whites only" fountain, I noticed someone had spit his gum out, and the chewed up wad was sitting in the drain.

"Have a great time, Roddy," said Mom, getting a little teary eyed.

"Don't do anything that would disgrace the family name," remarked Dad.

"What do you mean by that, Dad?"

"Oh, never mind. Say hi to Willie and Harry. Don't fall off of any horses or Brahma bulls. Make sure no one puts his branding iron on your butt," he laughed.

After a final hug, I climbed into the bus and presented the driver with my ticket. "I'll be around to take tickets in a while. Take a seat," he said gruffly.

I grabbed a window seat and hoped the other two seats in my row would stay empty. Passengers filed in. Most moved toward the back, stowing their packages in the overhead racks. My seat had a thick cushion and was quite comfortable. Ah, a lever to make it recline. I put my pack in the seat next to me and pushed back. "Not too bad," I thought, while looking out the window. There were my parents, holding hands as they turned the corner on the way back to the car. It was only much later when the thought occurred to me that my trip to Texas might be a little vacation for them, too. One less very active teenager to deal with.

A man sat down in front me and glanced in my direction. He sized me up and gave me a little smile and a nod as if to say, "Way to go, buddy. Traveling without your parents." He lit up a cigarette and dropped the match in the aisle. The familiar smell of tobacco pervaded the bus. After drawing in a long drag, the man slowly exhaled in my direction and then whistled out a fine stream of smoke. He finished by blowing out several small smoke rings. By lightly tapping his cheek he made tiny circles of smoke parade out of his mouth. What a showoff. As he sat down, he slapped a magazine on to the seat next to him. It was one of the coveted magazines covered in the mysterious brown paper wrapper.

The doors of the bus sighed shut, and we edged our way out of the Coral Gables Bus Terminal. Down Miracle Mile we drove, passing popular Saturday afternoon hangouts, the Miracle Theater and Jahn's Ice Cream Parlor. We headed east, down tree-lined Coral Way.

"Next stop, Miami, Florida," announced the driver through his microphone.

Several hours later, cruising north on the Greyhound, I looked out the window, happy to be on the open road. Palm trees and strip malls gave way to dairy farms, small lakes, swamps, and saw grass. It was wonderful to be away from home and away from the monotony of the Miami suburbs. We passed through quaint beach towns and villages with town squares and city halls. Miles and miles of orange groves lined the highway. It looked like millions of oranges were ready to be harvested.

Out the window a beautiful sunset turned the sky every color in the rainbow over the Everglades. The road took us past a large tranquil lake. A flock of wading birds stood on stick-like legs. Some were white. Some were pink. The last small segment of the setting sun was reflected in the water. Only the top arc remained above the horizon. It reminded me of an egg yolk sizzling in the pan. The sky turned orange, red and yellow, as the sun disappeared into the water. The colors of the crystal blue water and the golden yellow sky seemed to merge, and there was a momentary flash of green that reflected off the white clouds just above the horizon.

The sky turned dusky and then dark as night fell. We made a quick stop at Vero Beach, and several passengers grabbed their bags and stepped off the bus. A slim woman with very short hair and a tight skirt boarded and sat down in the row in front of me. She took the seat next to the man who had blown the smoke rings. He smiled and offered her a cigarette. Striking a match, he suavely lit her cigarette before lighting his own. As the bus pulled out of the station, they smoked and chatted. I perked up my ears and tried to eavesdrop on their conversation but could only hear a few words they exchanged. Cigarettes finished, the man reached across the woman and picked up the magazine that was on the aisle seat. I craned my neck as he tore off the brown paper wrapper. Oh my God. It was a *Playboy*.

They began leafing through the magazine, tittering as he slowly turned the pages. I swayed side to side trying to see what they were looking at, but without standing up, there was no way my curiosity would be satisfied. The woman leaned closer to the man and he placed his hand on the back of her neck and started gently caressing her. She turned her lips to his cheek and lightly kissed him. The man held the magazine out and unfolded the centerfold. He held it up high for her to see, so that there before me was a large color photograph of a naked woman. My eyes felt like they were popping out of my head. So much beautiful flesh. My buddies were right. A woman's body is the loveliest creation in the world. I thought. "I'm thirteen years old. How am I ever going to wait 'til I get married?"

As the couple continued to look at the magazine, I opened a comic book in an attempt to distract myself from thoughts of the *Playboy*. Archie had two girls. Lucky boy. Betty the blondie was crazy about him and would do anything for him. Archie had a dilemma: He couldn't take his eyes off raven-haired Veronica, the beautiful tease who was after the rich slickster Reggie. Archie followed Veronica around like a puppy. He was smitten. All she had to do was bat her eyes at him, and he became her slave. In Archie's love triangle, there were no winners. Everyone's love was unrequited. The comic was written with innocence and good humor. *However*, having just seen a *Playboy* centerfold, the adventures of Archie didn't hold my attention for long.

The bus got very quiet, and nearly everyone had turned off their reading lights and closed their eyes. The man and woman in the row in front of me closed the *Playboy* and wrapped their arms around each other. I could see that they were hugging and could hear the sound of them kissing. As the bus rolled on, they snuggled together like an adoring couple. My curiosity and imagination were aroused. It was a romance between two people on a bus between cities in the middle of the night. Are they total strangers? Are they married to other people? Do they love each other? Will they ever see each other again? Will I ever be able to get some sleep?

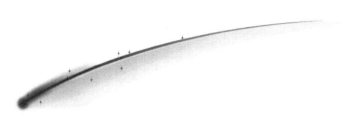

CHAPTER 4
MARY BETH AND JANIE

THE BUS STARTED to fill up with boarding passengers after a brief stop in Deland, a sleepy town in Central Florida. Two girls got on the bus and walked slowly down the aisle. They were carefully checking out the passengers as they approached my row. It looked like I was the only other young person riding the bus that night. "Can we sit here?" the younger girl asked me. "Sure. Why not?" I replied, feeling very pleased at the thought of sitting with girls about my age. "Do you mind if I have the window seat?" the older girl asked. "I like to look out the window."

"Fine", I said, stepping into the aisle to let her in.

"Janie, why don't you take the aisle seat?"

The three of us settled in. As the bus left the Deland bus station, I found myself sitting between two slim blonde girls with fair skin, very pretty faces, and exotic southern accents.

"Hi, there. I'm Mary Beth and that's my little sister, Janie. Her Christian name is Suella Jeanne, but everyone calls her Janie. What's your name?"

"My name is Rodger," I replied.

Maybe because I hadn't spoken to anyone since I boarded the bus in Coral Gables, words started to flow out of my mouth like oil gushing from a well. "Rodger is what my teachers and classmates call me. My mom likes to call me Roddy because when she was a girl she was a big fan of Roddy McDowell. Don't you think Roddy seems kind of babyish? Now that I'm a teenager, everyone calls me Rod. That's not too confusing, is it?" I babbled on.

"Pleased to meet you, Roddy," Mary Beth said with a sweet smile. "Janie and I are taking the bus home to Greenwood, Mississippi. We just spent two weeks visiting our grandpapa and grandmama. They live in New Smyrna Beach. We just love the beaches in Florida. We went swimming every day and got really brown. You should see my tan line. I have a whole bag full of shells for my collection. I just love playing in the waves, too. Next summer we want to come back and learn how to surf. Those surfer boys look dreamy. I had so much fun, I wouldn't care if I never went home."

"What are you doing on the Greyhound this late at night, Rodger?" asked Mary Beth, the older sister, as she leaned into me and our shoulders bumped together.

The bus went around a curve and I let myself lean in the other direction, now rubbing shoulders with Janie. She glanced at me and our eyes met for a second. She looked down at her hands and giggled just a little.

"I'm taking the bus from Miami to Dallas. I decided to use my bar mitzvah money to go visit my cousins in Texas. It's kind of an adventure. I love seeing new places. And now I've made two new friends—you two girls. I've never met anyone from Mississippi before," I replied.

"Bar mitzvah? What in the world is that? What a strange-sounding word," said Janie, stifling a giggle.

Before I could answer, we noticed an older black woman, maybe in her seventies, slowly limping down the aisle.

"Make it snappy back there, girl! We're on a schedule! Colored to the back of the bus. Hurry up now, girl! Move it!" barked the impatient bus driver through the microphone located next to the driver's seat.

The woman moaned with each step as she dragged herself toward the back, looking for an empty seat and a place to stow the heavy paper bag full of her belongings. She sighed and grunted as she collapsed into the seat across the aisle and one row behind us. The driver closed the door, and the bus pulled out of yet another Greyhound station and began rolling out of town.

"Can you believe Negroes have to sit in the back of the bus? The driver was completely rude and disrespectful to that woman. Don't you think all people are equally deserving of respect, no matter what the color of their skin? You know, we're not better than them just because we're white," I said, thinking that I might be getting just a little bit preachy.

"Well, that's just silly," said Mary Beth. "In Mississippi the colored know their place. Why I just love our housekeeper, Naomi. She's the sweetest thing and has taken care of us since we were babies. But she's different from us, and she knows it."

"Not really," I said. "No race is better than another. There are good whites and bad whites, good Negroes and bad Negroes. If they have equal opportunities with us, Negro children can grow up to be just as successful as we can. The Civil War has been over for almost 100 years. President Lincoln emancipated the slaves so many years ago, but black Americans still aren't truly free, even today."

"If you talked like that in Greenwood, you'd find yourself in trouble with the Klan. They'll fight to the death against integration. Negroes and white people in the same school? I can't imagine," said Mary Beth.

"Well, what do you think? Do you think segregation is fair? Do you think that bus driver should have been so disrespectful to that woman?" I asked.

"I don't really know. I know how things are in Mississippi, and no one ever questions it. I never heard a white boy talk like that before. I guess we should be nice to everyone," replied Mary Beth. "I guess I really don't know."

"Let's talk about something else," complained Janie. "What's a ba...bar mitzvah or whatever you called it? I just love *Babar the Elephant.* Mama used to read the Babar books to us when we were little girls."

"No, no. Not Babar. A bar mitzvah is what happens when a Jewish boy turns thirteen. It's a celebration of his becoming a man.

My bar mitzvah was last November. I led the service at temple and had a big party with all my friends and family. I racked up almost three hundred dollars in cash and some cool presents. Now I have a brand new Polaroid camera and a reel-to-reel tape recorder. Best presents ever."

"You're Jewish? You mean you're a Hebrew from the Old Testament? The chosen of God who rejected Christ and are damned to hell forever? I've never met a Jew before. You look normal enough to me, even if you have some pretty crazy ideas. People say Jews have horns like the devil. You don't have horns under that wavy blonde hair, do you?" asked a surprised Mary Beth, as she tousled my hair and examined my head for hidden horns.

Shivers ran down my spine from the touch of her fingers in my hair. My heart skipped a beat as I took a deep breath.

"Well, no horns, but what is that little bump in your forehead?" she asked, as she brushed away some hair that was hanging over my forehead.

"That's my smart bump. When we were little kids my parents bought us a little guitar. It was really a ukulele. It was my favorite gift ever, and I just played and played. It wasn't hard to pick out some simple melodies. My older sister kept asking for her turn to play with the uke, but I wouldn't part with that four string. She got so mad she grabbed it from me and cracked it over my head. That was the end of the uke, and the beginning of my bump. My head bled pretty bad, but Mom just put a band-aid on it and didn't take me for stitches. After I healed, this bump stayed on my forehead. My teachers call it my smart bump.

"Mom and Dad were not in a hurry to buy us a new guitar after the first one ended up cracked. So when I was ten, I traded a baseball bat and glove to a kid who had an old guitar but didn't know how to play it. It's been okay to strum chords and pick out melodies on. Wish I had a six string with a nice, easy action to play on. It'll take forever to save enough to buy a Gibson or a Martin."

Mary Beth tilted her head, smiled, and said, "So you're a smart boy, with soft, soft hair who plays guitar and believes in integration. That doesn't sound so devilish to me. Some of those Bible stories are so silly. I don't really think Eve was created from Adam's rib. Virgin birth? I sometimes wonder if Jesus really was the son of God."

"Both my Christian and Jewish friends back in Miami sometimes talk about the *Bible* and religion. We mostly agree that no one really has all the answers. The Bible stories we're taught in synagogue and church seem so childish. Some things will always remain mysteries. We all want to know what happens after we die. When I was a little kid I asked my Mom what happens after we die. She said, "Don't worry. Just like I was there to take care of you when you born, I'll be there to take care of you in the next life. The important thing is to not live in fear.""

"What a comforting answer. Your mom sounds very sweet and loving. I hope my mom will be there for me and Janie when we go to heaven."

I asked, "Mary Beth, don't you agree with Dr. Martin Luther King, the Negro Baptist minister, when he preaches that we are all God's children? Christian and Jews, whites and blacks, rich and poor are all equal in God's eyes."

"Excuse me, young man." The old Negro woman who had hobbled to the back of the bus was leaning forward from her seat behind me. "Are you a Freedom Rider down south here to help us with our struggle for equality? I heard you talking about integration and Dr. King. What college do you go to? Harvard?"

"I don't go to college, ma'am. I just finished the eighth grade."

"You sound like a wise young man, and I just want to shake your hand," she said as she reached forward and clasped my hand with her dry, calloused palms.

"I'm starting eighth grade this fall," interrupted Janie. "My last year of grammar school before I finally go to high school. I can't wait. Are you ready for high school, Rod?"

"I still have one more year of junior high. In Miami, we have to wait until tenth grade before we get to go to high school. Still, it's never too soon to start thinking about college.

My junior high is an obstacle course. It's full of tough guys and bullies. One time, I set the curve on a big science test. Since I made a perfect score, the science teacher called me up in front of the entire eighth grade and called me a science genius. He pinned a medal on my shirt and suggested that people give me a pat on the back when they saw me in the hall. I thought, 'Thanks for pinning a target on my back, Mr. Wizard.' It was like an invitation to get beaten up. Of course I ditched the pin immediately. For the rest of the day, I couldn't dodge all the fake congratulations on my status as a genius. Those back slaps started to get brutal. One guy nearly bruised me, pounding my back, saying, 'Nice going, Einstein.' Lucky for me, there's this guy at school who serves as my bodyguard. Wood the Hood lives next door, and we've been buddies since fifth grade. He loves hanging out at my house and eating Mom's cooking. The Woodman is a little crazy, and no one wants to mess with him. When he saw me surrounded by back-slapping idiots, Wood put his arm around me and said to my tormentors, 'When you're messing with the Noodleman, you're messing with the Woodman. When you're messing with him, you're messing with me. When you're messing with me, you're messing with him. Who wants to mess with the Woodman?' He lunged forward, shaking his clenched fists, and you never saw so many tough guys jump backward like startled cats. Then they escaped by slinking away. No one bugged the science genius after that. Wood's a little crazy, and when he fights, he will hurt you bad. He's probably a future convict, but Wood the Hood is always there for me. It's a good deal that the toughest guy in school is one of my best friends."

"I'm going into tenth grade. I just turned fifteen. The boys at Greenwood High fight a lot, too. I'm not supposed to be dating yet, but I have met up with some guys at the movie theater who wanted to sit with me at the movies. When the lights go down, they get kind of grabby with their hands," Mary Beth informed me.

"I've been on this bus eight hours now and haven't been able to sleep at all," I said while stifling a yawn and stretching out my arms.

"You poor baby," said Mary Beth, as she put her arm around me and pulled my head to her breast. She leaned her head against mine. "Let's all try to get some sleep."

Suddenly I was in heaven. My cheek was pressed against her soft, soft body. There was no way I was going to fall asleep. I closed my eyes and thanked God for this wonderful feeling. The material of her dress was smooth and sheer. Her silky hair was like angel wings falling over my face and smelled like flowers. I could feel her breast move up and down with each breath. Realizing that I was holding my breath, I slowly let the air out of my nose and hoped she could feel the warmth of my breath through her clothes. Please God, let this moment last forever, I prayed.

I felt the urge to move my head so my lips would be nearer to her breast but didn't dare. I nuzzled my cheek and nose against her as she began to run her fingers through my hair and pet me. Shivers, goose bumps, and an aching in my stomach and parts below began. This was the best moment in my life. There is no way I am going to fall asleep now. Minutes went by as I gloried in each breath and movement. Mary Beth rubbed the back of my neck for a moment and then let her hand relax against my side. She started breathing deeply and slowly. I let myself sigh.

The bus hit a bump the road, and we startled awake. I had never slept so soundly. My cheek was still against Mary Beth's breast, and on the other side of me I could feel Janie's thigh against mine. I slowly opened my eyes and looked down at the noticeable swelling in my pants. I turned slightly toward Janie and saw that she was also staring in the direction of my fly. "Is that because of me?" she asked.

I sat up immediately and crossed my legs, embarrassed to have been caught in my aroused state.

Mary Beth yawned and stretched. "Oh, that was restful. Did you get some sleep, too, Roddy, dear?"

"Uh huh," was all I could reply.

We traveled on through the night, each of us reading our own magazines and chatting a little bit. I savored each time I bumped up against the girls whenever the bus swayed around a curve.

Mary Beth took my hand and stroked it gently. We interlocked fingers.

"We are now crossing the Mississippi River," announced the bus driver. I looked down into the black water from the high bridge and saw the barges moving up and down the river. Dawn was breaking and I was finally in the West. In some ways I felt transformed.

Much too soon for me, the bus pulled into the Greyhound station in downtown New Orleans. "Last stop, New Orleans," said the bus driver.

"This is where we change for the bus to Greenwood."

"I change for Dallas here, too." I said, feeling regret that our journey together was at an end.

We gathered our things and made our way to the front of the bus. The three of us stood in front of the bus, staring at each other.

"Thank you, young man, for the things you said on the bus. God bless you," the old Negro woman said to me as she reached out and clasped my shoulder warmly.

"Rodger, I wish there was a boy like you back in Greenwood. It was a pleasure meeting you," said Mary Beth, as she put her arms around me and kissed me sweetly on the lips. Her lips tasted like honey. She lingered and let me kiss her back. My knees nearly gave way. My first kiss. It was unforgettable in every way.

Janie turned toward me and gave me a sweet smile. Her face turned very pink. She didn't say a word. The two southern belles turned and walked away. I watched them as they approached the bus station, knowing I would never see them again. They put their heads together whispering and giggling. Staying a few steps behind the girls, I headed into the station and looked for the information board. What time was the next bus leaving for Dallas, my final destination?

CHAPTER 5
NAWLINS

IT WOULD BE more than three hours before my bus pulled out for Dallas. The bus station was very busy, but also a little gloomy. Passengers were milling around waiting for their buses. Families sat on chairs and benches. Some seedy-looking people wearing worn and patched clothes were lying right on the bus station floor. There were travelers using their suitcases as pillows. It was surprising to see so many people who looked so poor. People in ragged clothes wandered around asking for spare change from the better-dressed people. A young man sitting in a corner played classical music on a violin. His tone was clear and sweet. His graceful bowing produced the familiar sound of "Canon in D" by Pachelbel. His upturned baseball cap lay on the floor in front of him. There were a few dollar bills and some change in it. This fine musician was playing the violin for tips. He nodded his thanks as I placed a dime in his hat.

I debated whether I should find a seat and read until my bus boarded or leave the dreary bus station and explore New Orleans. It was an easy decision. Enough of bus stations!

As soon as I stepped onto the street a car drove up and stopped at the curb right next to me. The driver leaned out the window and said, "Bootleg taxi. Take you anywhere in the Big Easy for fitty cent. I'll show you the French Quarter. It's a place where anything goes."

"My bus leaves for Dallas in a couple of hours. Can you show me the sights and get me back to the station on time?" I asked.

"I'm your man. I can show you anything and get you every-thing. Name's Marcel. Hop in and I'll take you for a ride. *Allons!*"

Marcel threw my bag in his trunk. I plopped down in the back-seat of his car. It didn't look like the kind of cab we sometimes took in Miami. The seat covers were torn, and there was a musty smell. Candy wrappers and cigarettes butts were everywhere. There was a crumpled up magazine on the seat next me. It was opened to a page that was titled "Personal Ads". I opened it and quickly scanned a few pages: "Men Seeking Women. Women Seeking Men. Men Seeking Men, Women Seeking Women". One ad read "Full-figured, caramel-skinned gal looking for a finan-cially secure gentleman." Another said, "Lonely professional man seeks female companionship." Another ad puzzled me. It read "Best Ball in the Quarter. Anything Goes. Call Pierre." It seemed to me that Pierre was trying to attract Cinderella to a ball so she could meet her handsome prince. New Orleans must be a city of fairy tales.

"Next stop, Bourbon Street," said Marcel, as we drove slowly down narrow streets. The old houses had balconies that extended over the sidewalks. Some of them looked ready to collapse. New Orleans felt like an older, more exotic, more historic city than Miami. As we approached the lights of the French Quarter, I could hear music growing louder. Marcel stopped at the turn onto Bourbon Street. A woman whose face was covered with makeup stuck her face in the car window. The smell of her perfume made me gag. She bent over in her faded red, low-cut dress, and I could see that she wasn't wearing any underwear.

"Marcel, does your fare want a ride with me?" asked the woman as she ran her hands suggestively over her hips.

"No baby, dis one just looking," Marcel replied with a familiar wink. He stroked his scraggly goatee.

"Okay, *mon cher.* Come back and see Fifi LaLane when you grow up," she said, as she threw me a kiss.

We slowly cruised down Bourbon Street. Musicians were playing at every street corner. A man in frayed pants and with a chapeau on his head was playing violin. His bow flew over the strings with great flair. A small crowd gathered around three guys playing electric guitars. They were plugged into small amps with tears in the grill covers. The bass player thumped out the power-ful melodic bass line of "Pipeline". The lead guitarist answered with a screaming riff. His fingers slid up and down the fret board effortlessly. They jammed hard. A skinny black guy in cutoffs and an open shirt was shaking a tambourine and banging rhythmi-cally on garbage can lids. The passing crowd was dancing to the music.

I asked Marcel to stop for a minute so I could listen to a Dixieland Band. A trumpet and clarinet harmonized as they played the tune "Five Foot Two, Eyes of Blue". I sang along as the familiar old song "Ain't She Sweet" rang out. A man in worn-out shoes tap-danced along with the music. He clicked his heels and he jumped so high. He tipped his derby hat to me. On the hat was a fleur-de-lis made of green rhinestones. I was way down yon-der in New Orleans, and the dreamy scene was like the Garden of Eden. It was kind of sad that these wonderful musicians were working for tips placed in their instrument cases and hats. No one was getting rich. But everyone was enjoying the music. I couldn't stop bobbing my head in time to the swinging beat.

There was a parade of happy people dancing down the middle of Bourbon Street. They strutted and pranced while several twirled parasols. Many wore tattered clothes but had colorful necklaces that swayed from side to side as they danced. What a party atmosphere. Couples strolled arm in arm down the street, and some were sipping drinks. This party looked like it would continue all day and all of the night. This was fun and unlike anything I had ever seen before. We drove by Preservation Hall, Jackson Square, Reverend Zombie's House of Voodoo, The Jazz Parlor, the Cat's Meow, the Coco Club, and the House of the Rising Sun. What went on behind those closed doors? I could only imagine. And believe me, I imagined a lot.

Out the window of the bootleg taxi, I saw a solitary man standing apart from the partying crowd. He was dressed in a tattered white robe. His long hair and beard were tangled and looked electrified. They were streaked with white and gray. He whipped his head in my direction and locked eyes with me. His bulging, bloodshot eyes had a wild, pleading look that pierced me. The sign he carried read "Sinners Repent! The End Is Near! Jesus Is Coming Soon!" Pointing his crooked finger directly at me, he commanded, "You must be saved, brother." Ignoring the prophet of doom, Marcel turned the corner and parked the taxi.

"Okay, Sonny, before I take you back to your bus, we'll make a quick stop, and I'll let you treat me to a Nawlins gastronomical specialty." We hopped out of the car and entered the Beignet Shop. The aroma of freshly baked delicacies made my mouth start to water. Marcel picked out two pastries, and I paid for them.

I bit into my beignet while Marcel savored his. It was the best doughnut I had ever tasted. It was crispy on top, covered with powdered sugar, and sweet and chewy in the middle. I bought another beignet to eat on the next leg of the bus ride.

"Okay, *mon ami*. It's time to get you back to the station. I don't want you to miss your bus. You just had the best tour of Nawlins fitty cent will ever buy. I hope you enjoyed your taste of the French Quarter. Come back some day for Mardi Gras. *Laissez les bon temps rouler. Au revoir. Bon chance*," said Marcel as he dropped me off in front of the Greyhound station.

By the time I returned to the station, my bus was already loading. After sampling a little of crazy, jive-jumping New Orleans, I knew that I wanted to come back someday and explore the clubs I was still too young to enter.

Away from home twenty-four hours, and I was having the time of my life. *Playboy* magazine, Mary Beth and Janie, Bourbon Street... The start of my summer vacation was opening my eyes to a new and wonderful world. I boarded the express Greyhound to Dallas.

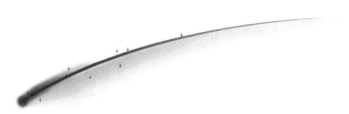

CHAPTER 6
TEX CONAWAY

THERE WAS AN empty row on the bus out of New Orleans. Settling into my window seat, I finished the last chapters of *Exodus*. The book left me outraged. Even at age thirteen I had been almost completely unaware of what happened to the Jewish people during World War II and in the years following the war. How could the Germans have hunted down and killed the Jews of Europe? These were the aunts, uncles, and cousins of my parents that had been exterminated. It was my good fortune that my grandparents left the old country as teenagers and came to the United States. Of course, they never saw their families again.

Exodus was the story of the survivors of the concentration camps and their struggle to leave Europe to live in the Jewish homeland that would become Israel. After the war the English detained the liberated Jewish victims of the Nazis in detention camps in Cyprus. The surviving remnants of European Jewry were denied entry to Israel by the English. They were trying to appease the Arabs from whom they bought oil. The story of the survivors of the Nazi horror huddled in the little boat they renamed Exodus, trying to reach the shores of the Jewish homeland touched and angered me. No wonder when my dad's war buddies would come over to swap war stories they would get quiet and whisper when the kids entered the room. The same thing happened when my grandparents gathered with their friends to talk about the people they left behind when they boarded ships and traveled in steerage across the Atlantic. They were just about my age when they left their parents for a new life in America. They probably knew that they would never see their loved ones again.

My sisters and I loved to listen to the old folks sing wistful tunes from the old country. There was sadness and nostalgia in their voices as they sang the Yiddish songs they had learned from their parents. Even now, almost twenty years since World War II ended, they didn't know the fate of many of their loved ones. They never heard from them again after the Nazis marched through Poland and the Ukraine, massacring every Jew they could get their hands on. All those years of Sunday school and Hebrew school and I didn't learn details about the attempt to kill all the Jews until I read Leon Uris's book. My bar mitzvah symbolized the beginning of my manhood, but part of my childhood innocence ended when I read *Exodus*.

Out the window on U.S. Highway 90 there were signs designating the road a hurricane evacuation route. After a couple hours of driving through the swampy bayou, we made a quick stop in Morgan City, Louisiana. The weather was very hot and very humid. Lightning flashed on the horizon. A sudden wind gusted, and I felt it blow through the window of the bus. Thunder crashed and echoed like cannons. It slowly rumbled and tumbled away. It seemed like fanfare for the very tall man now sauntering down the aisle of the bus. After giving me a quick glance he stopped at my row. He tossed an expensive looking briefcase into the overhead bin. It was a cowboy! A ten-gallon hat sat on top of his head. His pointed boots were spit shined. He even had on a little Texas string tie. Wow! I wasn't even in Texas yet and I was meeting a real cowboy.

"Howdy, son. Tex Conaway's the name. What's your name?" he asked as he took off his hat and sat down next to me.

"Rodger."

"Rodger what?"

"Rodger Noodleman."

"Where you from, son?"

"Miami."

"Miami Beach? Coral Gables? South Miami?"

"Yeah, yeah, sure," I replied, getting a little annoyed at the probing questions.

"You a Jewish boy?" he twanged.

I immediately put my hands up to my head. Was Tex going to check me for horns, too? "Uh...uh...uh..."

"That's okay, son. I'm Jewish myself. Real name is Benjie Cohen. They've been calling me Tex all my life. Changed the last name to Conaway for business purposes, you know. The oil business. I'm heading back to Austin, then up to Stonewall to my ranch. I grew up right there on the Pedernales River, on the land my granddaddy bought. We Cohens have been Texans for over one hundred years."

I shifted in my seat. I was sitting next to a Jew named Tex. A Jewish cowboy! He looked at the book that was resting on my lap.

"Ah. I see you're reading *Exodus.* Now that's a story I know something about. So many Jewish lives were snuffed out by the Nazis. Let me tell you a little-known piece of history that every American should know. Before and during the war, I worked with my old friend and neighbor, Lyndon Johnson, on Operation Texas. You see, American Jews and high government officials were aware that the Nazis were persecuting German Jews. After the Nuremberg laws were passed, depriving the Jews of Germany citizenship, we knew something had to be done to help the oppressed Jewish victims who were becoming desperate. We smuggled more than five hundred Jews out of Europe, across the Mexican border, and into Texas. Back in 1937, President Franklin D. Roosevelt put a young U.S. Congressman, Lyndon Baines Johnson, in charge of the project."

"Wow! You helped Lyndon Johnson smuggle Jews out of Nazi Germany and into Texas? That is incredible!"

"Oh yeah, Lyndon and I go way back," he continued. "We were friends and occasionally rivals back in high school. Ours was the only Jewish family around Johnson City. Congressman Johnson, still in his first term, called me up to help run the rescue project because he knew the Jewish community was frantically trying to get people out. I made eight trips to Mexico and Cuba, trying to save Jewish lives. Even flew to Europe and saw firsthand what those Nazi butchers did. Lyndon was a mighty big man. Smartest move he made was marrying Bird. She was quite a gal. From a prominent family and very, very smart.

"Back in my high school days I was a bit of a smart aleck. I used to tease Claudia Taylor about her nickname, Bird. Unfortunately she realized I was talking about the shape of her nose. Sort of like a bird's beak. Because I mocked her a little there was some tension between us. But Lyndon fell in love with her and always used the nickname Lady Bird. She was a lovely and classy young woman. I had no doubt this powerful young couple was bound for success."

"You teased Lady Bird Johnson about her nose? You've got to be kidding me, Mr. Conaway."

"Nope, I'm not kidding. But I do still regret it. After they got married, Lyndon and Bird used her daddy's money and bought a radio station. They realized how huge TV was going to become and bought a TV station too. When Lyndon was in the Senate, he used his influence to build a communications monopoly that made them millions of dollars. Now that he is vice president of the United States, every dirt road in and around Johnson City is being paved and illuminated with streetlights. You can believe me, Lyndon always takes care of the folks who helped him get his start in politics.

"Lyndon and Lady Bird knew how to build a political base and accumulate wealth and power. In Congress, it didn't take Lyndon long to rise into a leadership position. The man had an enormous ego. He wanted everyone in his family to have his initials. Lyndon not only made sure his wife and daughters shared his initials; he even named his dog Little Beagle Johnson. Can you believe that?"

"Sounds like you know just about everything about Vice President Johnson, Mr. Conaway," I replied in admiration.

"With LBJ as vice president of the United States of America, I can assure you that we Jews have a friend in very high places. Lyndon's grandpa, Samuel Johnson, was friends with my *zaydeh*,

Isidore Cohen. Grandpa Johnson was a Christodelphian. That's a Christian sect that believes the Jews are the chosen of God. Grandpa Sam told Lyndon, 'Take care of the Jews, God's chosen people. Consider them your friends and help them any way you can.' You can be sure Lyndon took that to heart. He is a fine man who cares about all Americans, no matter what religion or color they are."

"Don't you think it's remarkable that a Southern politician was able to get elected while being in favor of civil rights? I asked.

"Yes, and Lyndon is a remarkable man. JFK never could have won the election without him on the ticket. President Kennedy, a Catholic from Massachusetts, carried Texas and five other southern states. Those old rebels still wouldn't vote for a Republican, even if his name was Jesus Christ. Their memories are long. They'll never forget that Abe Lincoln sent William Tecumseh Sherman to burn the South one hundred years ago.

"I'll tell you what. Many of these good old white Texas boys aren't any too happy about what's going on now in Washington, D.C. My granddaddy came to Texas to escape religious persecution in Poland. Their granddaddies came to Texas after fighting in the Civil War for the Confederacy. When they see a black man, they want him to cut the firewood and haul the water. I hear the Ku Klux Klan is more active now than it has been in years. I'm sure those sheet-wearing racists are up to no good. There is weaponry being hoarded and crimes being plotted in secret places in Texas. Change comes hard in this part of the world. Texas still is part of the Wild West. Now Lady Bird is traveling all over America trying to help Negroes achieve freedom and break down the old barriers of segregation."

"Yes," I interrupted. "It does seem ridiculous that the bathrooms in the bus stations are segregated and that Negroes can't drink out of a public water fountain. We treat blacks in the United States like second-class citizens, sort of like the Nazis did with the Jews."

Tex continued, obviously enjoying having a captive audience. "I hear very ugly things being said about how JFK and LBJ will never win a second term in 1964. Some powerful people who'd like to turn back the clock on civil rights in this country have made threats against them. Did you know Lyndon is the third man named Johnson to become vice president? Richard M. Johnson was vice president under President Martin Van Buren. Abraham Lincoln's vice president, Andrew Johnson, became the seventeenth president of our country after that proslavery Confederate John Wilkes Booth put a bullet in the head of the Great Emancipator. They have many enemies, but no one should underestimate the political or survival instincts of either Jack or Lyndon."

"So Vice President Johnson worked to help the Jews during World War II. That's a very interesting history lesson, Mr. Conaway."

"Just call me Tex. Everyone does."

As we drove through Louisiana and into Texas, Tex had something to teach me about every little town and village. We made stops in Lafayette, Lake Charles, Orange, Port Arthur, Beaumont, and Houston. The bus stations all looked pretty much the same. Driving farther west into Texas, the countryside began to turn from green to tan. The pine forests of eastern Texas became scarce. Soon we were traveling through dry prairie land. We passed by ranches that seemed to stretch for miles. Cattle grazed in the fields between oil rigs.

"See those oil rigs, Rodger? Oil has made Texas a very rich state. So many Texans struck it rich when gushers were found on their land. Millions and millions of dollars have been made. Huge oil reservoirs have also been discovered in the Gulf of Mexico, and there are oil rigs pumping it up from under the water. There is enough oil located under the floor of the Gulf to last our country for hundreds of years. In the 1930s it was the Texas Company that developed the steel barges that made drilling in deeper water possible. Now there are dozens of oil rigs visible off the shores of Texas and Louisiana. America needs oil to keep the wheels of commerce turning. The free enterprise system makes America great, and oil makes Texas rich. We need to drill, baby, drill."

As we drove into Austin, Tex pointed out the State Capitol. "That structure over there is the largest State Capitol in the U.S.A. Look at the beautiful rotunda. It's even taller than the Capitol in D.C. We do things big in Texas. Our governor is John Connally. He is an old friend of Lyndon's and campaigned for him against Kennedy for the Democratic presidential nomination in 1960. After Lyndon became vice president, he asked President Kennedy to appoint John Secretary of the Navy. Just last year he got elected governor of Texas. With Lyndon and John B.Connally, Jr. elected to such high offices, I'm sure the Democrats will control Texas politics for many years to come. Over there's the University of Texas. That magnificent tower you see is three hundred and seven feet tall. If you go up on the observation deck, you have the finest view in all of Travis County. You can see the campus and even the students walking to class. The city of Austin is visible in every direction. On a clear day, you can see all the way to the Texas Hill Country, where I live.

"Look over there. There's the football stadium. Football fans in these parts are singing, '*I don't care 'bout my gas and oil. As long as I got my Darrell Royal.*' Coach Royal has the Longhorns playing the best football in the country. Don't mess with the Horns and don't mess with Texas. Hook 'em Horns."

As we pulled into the Austin Greyhound station, Tex said, "This is the last stop for me, partner. It was a pleasure meeting you. Have a great time in the greatest state of them all. Watch out for those sweet little Texas rosebuds. I'll bet one or two of those purdy young gals would like to meet a boy like you."

"Bye, Tex. It was great getting to know you and learning some Texas history." I watched him duck his head so his ten-gallon hat would fit under the bus door as he exited the bus and strutted into the Austin bus station.

"All aboard. Greyhound bus number 1836 now leaving express to Dallas with stops in Temple, Troy, Waco, and Waxahachie. All aboard for Dallas, Texas."

CHAPTER 6

It only took a few hours to drive from Austin to Dallas. Two days after leaving Coral Gables, I stepped off the bus in Big D.

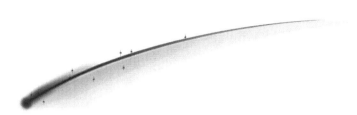

CHAPTER 7
MARILYN AND SUZY

"WELCOME TO DALLAS and welcome to our house. It's a little creaky, and the foundation is still settling, but we call it home," said Aunt Betty, as we pulled into the driveway. "I'm a little creaky, too, and I guess you could say my foundation is starting to settle as well," she laughed.

Aunt Betty was wearing a polka-dotted muumuu and still had a few curlers in her hair. She had crow's feet in the corner of her eyes and looked a bit careworn. She smiled warmly and gave me a motherly hug.

"It's going to be wonderful having a young man around the house. Marilyn and Suzy have been counting the days 'til you got here. Take your suitcase and backpack out of the trunk, and I'll show you which room you'll be sleeping in. You must be exhausted. Take a nap if you like."

"Thanks, Aunt Betty. I only slept a few minutes the whole bus trip from Miami. But I'm so excited to be here I don't think I'll be able to take nap right now."

Just then a car pulled up in front of the house.

"Oh wonderful. Marilyn and Suzy are just getting back from drill team practice. They'll be so happy that you're finally here," said Aunt Betty as my cousins Marilyn and Suzy got out of the back seat of a Buick filled with girls in their bright blue drill team uniforms.

"Bye, guys. Thanks for the ride. See you tomorrow," said Marilyn as she bounced over to me, sizing me up."

"Say hello to your cousin Rodger. He just got off the bus from Miami," said Aunt Betty.

"Hey there. You've shaped up nicely since the last time I saw you. I remember you as a four-year-old little weenie named Roddy who wouldn't stop crying because I wouldn't let you down from the top of the teeter-totter," laughed Marilyn.

"You were the sadistic cousin who wouldn't stop teasing me? That was nine years ago, and I still remember being tortured." We both moved forward for a hug, hesitated at the same time, and then gave each other an awkward squeeze.

"Hi, Roddy. Welcome to Dallas," said my pretty fourteen-year old cousin Suzy. Her front teeth stuck out just a little bit, but her smile was warm and friendly, and her complexion was clear and had a rosy glow. "So what name should I call you, Roddy or Rodger? asked Marilyn.

"Well, the family still calls me Roddy, but at school the teachers and most of the kids call me Rodger. Most of my friends call me Rod, but please don't call me Rodney," I babbled.

"So many names for my young cousin. I will be calling you Rodya after the villain in *Crime and Punishment*, Rodya Raskalnikoff," laughed Marilyn.

Tired of holding my backpack, I started to sling it over my shoulder. It slipped out of my hands, and I dropped it. Out popped an *Archie* comic book.

"I just finished Dostoevsky, and you're reading *Archie*? I think I'll be calling you Jughead," Marilyn teased.

"If you call me Jughead, then I'll call you Jugs," I responded, sizing up the shapely Marilyn in her tight-fitting dark blue drill team outfit.

"Don't get fresh with me, you weenie," Marilyn said as she grabbed me and put me in a headlock.

After escaping from the headlock, I gave my cousin a gentle slap on the behind. She shoved me toward her bedroom.

"This is my room, but you get it all for yourself. I'll be bunking with Suzy. Get unpacked and make yourself comfortable," said Marilyn.

I checked out the bed and put down my bags. My own room. That was a first for me. What luxury. My whole life I had shared a bedroom with my brother or one of my sisters. Wow. Privacy, and the privilege of being a male guest in a house full of girls. The room looked like it belonged to a typical but smarter than the average teenage girl. Marilyn had posters of Elvis and James Dean over her bed. A Dallas Cowboys pennant was taped to her mirror. I was surprised to see a New Yankees pennant hanging on the back of her door. There was an interesting selection of books on her shelves. *Catcher in the Rye, One Flew Over the Cuckoo's Nest, To Kill a Mockingbird, Flowers for Algernon,* and *The Diary of Anne Frank* were all titles that I recognized but hadn't read yet. On her desk was a certificate that she had won for Outstanding English Student at Thomas Jefferson High School. Her drill team batons were leaning against the wall in the corner.

I flipped on the clock radio, lay down on the bed, and closed my eyes. The Beach Boys were singing Brian Wilson's "In My Room" just for me. No one would ever sing harmonies as sweetly as the Beach Boys. I hummed along and began to daydream.

A few minutes later, I was startled by a very strange rhythmic noise coming from the front of the house. Curious, I went back out to the living room to see what it could possibly be. There were Marilyn and Suzy marching around in circles. Clomp, clomp, clomp.

"Check out these new boots. They're cute but so uncomfortable. It's going to take days to get used to them," Marilyn said to me.

The boots were white with bright blue pom-poms at the toe. I also took a good look at their tight-fitting drill team outfits with very short skirts that highlighted their cute figures.

"Suzy, can you believe that assistant drum major Todd at inspection this morning? I was wearing my chai necklace, and he told me I couldn't wear it because it isn't part of the uniform. He fingered the necklace, and I swear he tried to look down my blouse. I should have slapped him across the face."

"Marilyn, you know he's had a crush on you for two years. You'd think he'd give up by now," responded Suzy.

"Crush? I'll crush him with the heel of this boot," Marilyn threatened with a mischievous gleam in her eye.

"I wish a guy would pay attention to me the way they do to you," complained Suzy.

"Never fear, Suzy dear. You are fresh meat at TJ High. I'm sure those band nerds will be hitting on you in no time. Besides, you can't miss. You're my sis."

"Marilyn," whined Suzy.

"Hey. Get out your rifle. Let's show Roddy our drill team routine," said Marilyn.

They pulled out pieces of wood shaped like rifles and slung them over their shoulders.

"They don't let us take the real rifles home with us, but we do get real rifles for parades and football games," said Suzy. "Unloaded, of course."

"Here, Rod. Take mine. I'll give the commands, and you just follow orders," said Marilyn, as she handed me the mock rifle.

"Atten...HUT! PRE-SENT arms! Right shoulder arms! Left shoulder arms! At ease!" commanded Marilyn.

I obeyed and was just a half step behind Suzy, as she crisply performed the commands.

"Again! This time together. Atten...HUT! Right shoulder arms! Left shoulder arms! At ease! Much better. You're a natural, Rod," Marilyn laughed. "Suzy, show Rod how to twirl that rifle."

Suzy held her rifle in her left hand, pushed the top of it so it rotated, then pushed the bottom, and grabbed it again with her left hand, completing one rotation.

"Now you try it, Rod," said Suzy.

I imitated her motion but lost my grip on the wooden weapon. "Ouch! Right on my toe," I said, reaching down to rub my foot and pick up the rifle.

"That's why we wear these stiff boots. We might get blisters on our heels and ankles but no bruised toes," laughed Marilyn. "Now do it again."

Again I imitated Suzy's smooth motion of twirling the rifle like a baton. I was amazed when it ended up back in my left hand after one smooth rotation. After more practice, I was twirling the rifle with ease. The Woodman, back in Miami, would roll on the floor laughing if he could see me now.

"All right, Rodya! You're a natural with a rifle. No guys allowed on the drill team, but someday you'll make a fabulous soldier. We'll get you a shotgun and a six-shooter and turn the bar mitzvah boy into a regular Texas cowboy. Yee haw!"

"My feet are killing me. Let's get out of these uniforms and into comfortable clothes. Roddy, why don't you get yourself unpacked and comfortable? Mom will expect you for dinner on time at six o'clock," said Suzy. "Hope you like spaghetti and meatballs. C'mon, Marilyn, let's make a big salad and put lots of good stuff in it. I'm going to toast some garlic bread, too."

"Those meatballs smell great. I can't wait for a home-cooked meal and to sleep in a bed. It was a long bus ride from Miami. I kind of just ate candy and hot dogs at the bus stations. The only vegetables I've eaten in two days were french fries and ketchup."

CHAPTER 8
MICKEY MANTLE

A KNOCK ON MY door caused me to roll over in my sleep. "Wake up. Time to wake up. You've been snoring like Rip Van Winkle for twelve hours. We're not going to let you sleep all day." It was Marilyn, rarin' to go.

"I want to take you for a ride. I got my license last month, and I'm a great driver. We are going to cruise. It's time for you to see some Dallas hot spots. You're in Big D, little A, double L, A, S."

I jumped out of bed and was ready to go in a flash. It was unusual for me to sleep so late. Rested and refreshed, I was ready to explore a new city with my cousins.

"First, let's go for some breakfast. I'll get the keys, and we are out of here. Come on, Suzy Q. Make it snappy, Rodya."

We piled into the family's Ford Galaxy, and Marilyn turned the ignition. Grinding noises came from under the hood, but finally the car started up.

"We have three top forty stations here," said Marilyn as she quickly pushed the buttons on the radio to check what was playing on each station. "All right. Rock and roll on all three stations!" She chose one to listen to. Then she turned the volume dial all the way up as the speakers rattled and hissed.

On the radio Lesley Gore sang her hit song "It's My Party." She was crying because her best friend Judy stole her boy friend Johnny out from under her nose.

"Careful backing up," Suzy cautioned, as Marilyn shifted from reverse into first gear and we headed down Timberview Drive.

Smoothly letting the clutch in and out, Marilyn showed that she was getting used to shifting gears. She came to a full stop at the stop sign, and then went through the gears again up to a comfortable thirty miles per hour.

"I'd cry, too, if my best friend left my party wearing my boyfriend's ring," said Suzy.

"Look, Rod. On your left is Mickey Mantle's house. He's the best baseball player in the world. I just love his Oklahoma accent."

We slowly drove by a really big ranch-style house with a great looking Jungle Gym and a huge sliding board that led directly into a large swimming pool. There was even a batting cage and a pitching machine.

"Have you ever seen him?" I asked.

"Oh sure. He's a great neighbor. Everybody in Dallas loves Mickey," Suzy said. "I'm a huge Yankees fan. They pay Mickey one hundred thousand dollars a year. He's much better than Roger Maris, don't you think?"

"Maris hit sixty-one home runs and broke Babe Ruth's record, and I am partial to guys named Roger. However, it is my humble opinion that Mickey Mantle is one of the greatest baseball players ever. He is a great outfielder and a switch hitter, too. You're so lucky that he lives near you."

"Rodya, I've been on the phone all morning. The girls on the drill team want to know everything about you. They want to know if my Miami cousin is a great surfer. It must be great living in Surf City."

"Oh sure, I'm a regular beach boy. I catch a big wave whenever the surf's up. Someday I'm going to find myself a surfer girl, too." I crooned my favorite lyrics from Jan and Dean's "Surf City": *Two girls for every boy*.

"Do you like to shoot the curl?" asked Marilyn as we pulled into a parking lot. Marilyn parallel parked expertly and grinned triumphantly.

"Sure. Occasionally I wipe out in the barrel of an epic wave," I replied with false modesty. "Maybe some fine day I'll make it to Hawaii and surf the really big waves with the Big Kahuna and Duke Kahanamoku."

"I love driving. Suzy, can you believe I'm driving us to Orange Julius? And can you believe Mom let us have the car for the whole day? Freedom! I swear someday I'm going to make enough money to buy my own car."

We walked up to the beverage stand. "Three Orange Juliuses," ordered Marilyn.

"I want strawberry banana," said Suzy.

"Okay make it two Orange Juliuses and one strawberry banana. Have you ever had a Julius before? You're in for a treat."

The man behind the counter wearing a tall chef's cap poured orange juice and powdered sugar into the blender and whipped it up with a loud roar. It was orange, bubbly, and delicious. I drank mine down in a single slurp.

"Yummy. I wish we had Orange Julius in Miami. I want another one. I'll treat," I said.

"Great! Two more Orange Juliuses and another strawberry banana."

"Marilyn, I want triple berry this time," corrected Suzy. "Okay. Change the strawberry banana to a triple berry," she said to the juice man.

We drank the second drink, only this time I drank it slowly and savored each delicious gulp. I contemplated ordering a third. Before I put my glass down, Marilyn spoke up.

"Rodya, dahlink, do you like to bowl? We must keep you entertained."

"Oh sure, I bowl in the Saturday morning league at Bird Bowl in Miami. My team finished in second place last year. There is a big trophy with my name on it sitting above our fireplace on the mantle."

"Hey, I've got an idea. Let's go to Mickey Mantle Lanes," said Suzy.

"Yes, let's go to Mickey's place. It's just around the corner," answered Marilyn.

"Mickey Mantle has a bowling alley? I definitely want to go Mickey's lanes. Maybe we'll see Mickey himself," I said hopefully.

"I'll bet I can beat you both. I'm a much better bowler than Marilyn. I think I'm going to go out for the bowling team at TJ," bragged Suzy.

Leaving Orange Julius, Marilyn drove us to Mickey Mantle Lanes and parked the car like an expert. Inside the bowling alley, country western music blared from loudspeakers. There were autographed pictures of Mickey Mantle on the walls. A framed New York Yankees uniform with the number seven was prominently displayed. We sat down on the benches near our lane and changed into bowling shoes.

"I'm keeping score." Suzy said as she grabbed the pencil and wrote down our names on the score sheets. Mickey Mantle Lanes had it set up so the score was projected on a screen everyone could see.

"Rod, you go first. Then Marilyn. I'm going last," Suzy said as she neatly printed out our names.

I stepped to the line for my first frame. I made a smooth approach and then cranked the ball as hard as I could. Right in the pocket with plenty of action. Strike! I bowed deeply to Marilyn and Suzy, as I skipped back to my seat triumphantly.

Marilyn picked up her ball and made her approach awkwardly. Swinging her arm across her body, she rolled the ball into the left gutter. She straightened up a little on her second ball and managed to knock off three pins.

"My turn," said Suzy as she picked up her ball. She glided to the line and stroked the ball right into the pocket. "Aw, darn it. I left the ten pin standing."

The ball boy rolled the ball back to the ball return. On the second ball, Suzy carefully lined herself up and picked up the spare gracefully.

We bowled several more frames. I was throwing the ball as hard as I could, but my accuracy was suffering. I picked up another strike and a spare but had three open frames.

Marilyn had no luck. When she wasn't putting the ball into the gutter, she was getting splits. She wasn't even close to picking up one. She seemed a bit bored by the game. A group of high school kids walked up to a lane at the other end of the bowling alley.

"Oh my God. It's Jerry Nelson. Eye See Bee," moaned Marilyn.

"Eye See Bee?" I repeated.

"Icey Bee, Icey Bee, Icey Bee."

"Icey Bee? What are you talking about?

"ICB, ICB. I crave his bod. I crave his bod. Look, he's with two cheerleaders. He's the one." She was whining now and sounding a little babyish.

"Go say hi to him if you like him," I suggested.

"Don't even look over there. He doesn't even notice me. He barely knows that I exist," Marilyn said. She was certainly not her usual confident self.

"Hey, Marilyn," said Jerry with a wave across the bowling alley.

"Jerry, hey," she answered back, looking a little flustered.

Jerry turned back to the girls who were fawning all over him. He had his hand on the round derriere of one of the girls. She was leaning in to his body. He didn't even glance back toward our lane.

"Jerry Nelson is the star of the baseball team and a straight-A student. Marilyn has been mooning over him for months," Suzy quietly informed me.

"He's the one," whined Marilyn. "Look at him with his hand on that cheerleader's tush. Whenever I hear the Essex sing 'Easier Said Than Done', I know they're talking about me and Jerry. I'd be happy to sing to him, swing to him, or do anything for him to let him know that I love him, but it's easier said than done. Look at him. He loves those blondes with the great figures. ICB. But I don't have a chance with him. Why do I love him so?"

"Marilyn, don't you notice how the guys always check your form when you walk into a room? Don't be miserable. I'm sure there are a bunch of guys that like you and wish you were their girlfriend." It really made me feel sad to see my playful cousin so unhappy.

"ICB. Sometimes Jerry is all I can think about. The problem is when I see him, I get all timid and shy," she said with her mouth turned down in a pout.

"I guess we can't control who we love. It sometimes seems to me that girls are all I think about. I hope the girl I fall in love with will love me back. I don't ever want to break anyone's heart, but I really never want to have my heart broken."

"Roddy, you are wise beyond your years. You have no idea how it feels to love Jerry. Thanks for being sweet to me."

Marilyn got up again to bowl. She rolled it halfheartedly down the alley. The ball weakly hit the head pin on the nose. It looked like she was going to roll a split. Slowly the pins tottered and fell. Finally the ten pin toppled over. Miraculously, Marilyn had bowled a strike.

"That strike is for Jerry. He's the one."

We came to the tenth frame. I had no chance of catching Suzy. I was going to need a strike to keep it respectable. Marilyn was hopelessly behind. I slammed the ball hard down the alley but ended up missing a tough spare in the last frame. Suzy lined herself up for her tenth frame. She stroked the ball down the alley for a perfect strike.

"Okay. Feeling good now," said Suzy. She picked up the ball that the ball boy had sent back down to her. Sweet stroke and bingo! Another strike. Once again the pin boy set them up. The ball boy rolled the ball back. After it clanked hard against the other balls, Suzy picked it up and walked to the lane with confidence. She repeated the same smooth stroke she used with the last two balls. The ball rolled right into the pocket with impressive action.

"Three strikes in a row! Turkey! All right! 196. My best game ever. I told you I'd win."

"You definitely need to go out for the bowling team. I think if you try hard you can letter in bowling," Marilyn advised her sister, who was all smiles.

"I'm going to go check out that candy machine. Do you want anything?" I asked Marilyn and Suzy.

"I'll have some Milk Duds," said Marilyn.

"Clark Bar for me. Thank you," said Suzy.

The candy machine was in a dark corner near the water fountain and bathrooms. The carpet was very worn and sticky from the many drinks that had been spilled on it. There was chewed-up gum stuck to the wall. A round-shouldered guy was hunched over the pinball machine, rapidly tapping on the flippers. I walked over to the candy machine and started fishing in my pockets for some change.

"Let me buy you some candy," said the strange-looking guy who had left the pinball machine and snuck up on me. He threw one arm around me while trying to put his dime into the candy machine. He pulled the lever and out popped a package of Lifesavers. Handing the Lifesavers to me, he said, "Want some more candy? I'll buy you whatever you want."

I felt sorry for the guy. He looked like someone who didn't have many friends. I became very uneasy as he leaned closer to me. His teeth were yellow and brown and had wide spaces between them. Then I got a nauseating whiff of his foul-smelling breath.

"No, buddy. I changed my mind. I don't want any candy." I pulled his arm off of me and ducked away from him. I started walking back to the lanes where the girls were waiting for me.

A man who had been bowling put down his bowling ball and walked over to me in a hurry. "Don't let that guy buy you candy," he warned. "That guy is a queer. Don't take candy from him. Do you hear me?"

"He did seem kind of queer," I said as I hurried away. I was sure I didn't want to make conversation with another strange man I didn't know. I returned to where Marilyn and Suzy were sitting.

"Where's my candy?" said Marilyn.

"All I got were these Lifesavers. You can have them. A strange guy bought them for me. A man told me he's a queer and I shouldn't let him buy me candy."

The girls looked over at the candy machine. "Oh, him. I think he's what they call a switch hitter. Just like Mickey Mantle," laughed Suzy.

"I heard some guys at school threatened to hit him over the head with a baseball bat," Marilyn informed me. "I think they might really do it."

"He's really ugly and strange. But why do they want to beat him with a bat?" I asked.

"He's a queer. A *fagele*. He does stuff with boys. Blond cutie, you're just his style."

I didn't really know what Marilyn meant.

"Marilyn, it's getting late. We'd better go. We have to help Mom get ready for the unveiling Sunday. Everybody's coming to our house for a huge brunch after they get back from the cemetery. Rod, you'll get to meet a bunch of your Texas cousins. I can't believe it's been a year since Shuki died." Her mouth turned down into a sad pout. Choking up a little, Suzy whispered with a sob, "I miss my uncle so much."

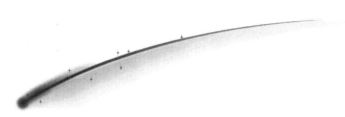

CHAPTER 9
DRILL TEAM

"**T**HEY'RE HERE. LET'S go," said Suzy, as a Ford station wagon pulled up.

"Wow. A Woody!" I exclaimed, noting the wood paneling along the sides. "This car is a real surfer's dream. I sometimes see the Woodies lined up in the parking lot near the pier in South Beach when the surf's up. The colorful surfboards are either sticking out the back window or in the rack on the roof. My dream is to own a Woody when I'm old enough to drive. Then I can drive all my surfin' friends to the beach when the big ones are rolling in."

"This is my surfer boy cousin visiting from Florida. I call him Rodya. I refer to him as Jughead if he doesn't obey my every command," Marilyn teased.

"Uh, I'd appreciate it if you would call me Rodger," I said, as I squeezed into the backseat next to a cute member of the drill team in her red and blue uniform.

"So you're from Surf City USA. Great to meet you. No surf anywhere near Dallas. It's a long drive to Galveston, and the waves there are usually puny," said the girl who was driving.

"Yep, like the song says, *'Two girls for every boy,'*" I sang enthusiastically. "I don't like those odds at all," replied Marilyn. "How about two boys for every girl?"

"Two boys for every girl. That's more like it," piped up the beautiful girl sitting next to me. Her blonde hair was short in a pixie cut that seemed to accent her adorable dimples. She smiled at me and gave me a knowing wink.

"I'd settle for one nice sweet boy who only liked me," said Suzy.

"That Donny Taylor sure was paying mucho attention to you at practice last week. You know that freshman tromboner with the crooked teeth and freckles," said the girl from the front seat.

"Tromboner! Tromboner! That's hysterical. That's what he gets when he's near my sister," howled Marilyn.

"Marilyn, shut up or I'll never speak to you again. Ignore her, Roddy."

I loved being in the car with all these girls. It was like entering the secret inner sanctum of the female. The girls I knew at home didn't talk like this—at least not around me.

Again coming from the front seat, "Hey y'all, did you hear about Linda Lou Lassiter? She was making out with her boyfriend, and the wires on their braces got locked together. They could not figure out how to get them apart. Linda Lou's mom had to take them to her dentist with them sitting in the car, lips together. The dentist had to cut the wires to separate them. It was so embarrassing, plus her lips got cut by the sharp ends of the wires."

"Nuh uh. You're making that up. No way that could have happened. You're just teasing me because I'm supposed to get my braces put on in a couple of weeks," said Suzy covering her mouth with her hands.

"Cross my heart, hope to die. Everybody's talking about it."

"We're here," Marilyn announced as the car pulled into the school parking lot. "Looks like everyone's already out on the field. Follow me, Rodya."

As we got out of the car, the lovely girl who had been sitting next to me reached out her hand to shake mine. "Hi, I'm Debbie."

"Rodger from Miami, at your service," I replied, feeling my ears burning just a little bit. She turned and ran off to join her fellow twirlers. I couldn't help but notice her long, slender legs and how her short hair bounced as she ran.

The field next to the school was full of activity. The drill team lined up next to the marching band. The football team was running scrimmages on the other side of the field.

The cheerleaders were in their blue and red uniforms, practicing cheers near the team. They shouted and kicked their legs high in the air. I walked over to the assembled drum line. The snare drummers were horsing around, practicing drum rolls and cadences. The bass drummers and tom-tommers were pounding out a marching beat. Being a drummer in my junior high band, I already knew dozens of marching cadences that my high school band used.

"Hey, I'm Marilyn's cousin Rod, visiting from Miami. I'm a drummer, and I dig that sound. Show me that cool beat you were playing."

Ricky tick. Rat a tat a tat tat tat. Paradiddle paradiddle, flam flam flam. Tripleparadiddle tripleparadiddle flam flam flam!

"Wow. I like that sound. Let me try it."

One of the drummers handed me his sticks, and I imitated their cadence. Ricky tick. Rat a tat a tat tat tat. Paradiddle paradiddle, flam flam flam. Tripleparadiddle tripleparadiddle flam flam flam! Then I showed them a few of the drum cadences from my school. Rat a tat tat tat, rat a tat tat tat, roll roll flam flam. Rat a tat tat tat, rat a tat tat tat, roll roll flam flam

"Hey that's a really neat beat. Always good to try something new. Maybe we'll use your cadences when we march at the state fair. So you're from Miami? Do you surf?"

"Yeah, yeah, sure. I surf all the time."

"Two girls for every boy," he sang. "That sounds like the proper ratio. I want to be a surfer, too. And you're staying with Marilyn and Suzy. This guy's got it made," he said to the other percussionists who had gathered around me.

"Band, listen up. Enough of this noise. Fall in. We have a halftime show to learn," shouted the drum major. He blew his whistle and the band started playing:

The eyes of Texas are upon you,
All the live-long day.
The eyes of Texas are upon you,
You cannot get away.

Do not think you can escape them,
At night, or early in the morn'
The eyes of Texas are upon you,
'Til Gabriel blows his horn.

While the band played, the drill team marched through their routine. Marilyn and Suzy twirled their rifles expertly. Other girls marched with Texas Lone Star flags and still others with the Stars and Bars of the Confederacy. The soloist twirled her baton behind her back. She threw it high in the air and caught it expertly, like one of those jugglers on the Ed Sullivan show. It was a colorful scene. High school football in Texas looked like a blast. At the end of the song, everyone shouted, "Go Rebels Go!"

The band and drill team moved through several more formations. I marveled at how tight they were. They made very few mistakes, and very few rifles were dropped. The band marched with precision, eight steps to every five yards. The band captain shouted, "Guide, guide. Keep your ranks clean." Their lines were nearly perfectly straight. I was very impressed. The drum major blew his whistle, and the assembled marchers came to a halt. Then they played their school song, "Dixie".

I wish I was in the land of cotton,
Old times there are not forgotten,
Look away, look away, look away,
Dixieland.

When the band finished playing "Dixie," the drum major shouted to the assembled group. "Great practice! Band dismissed. Go Rebels!"

"Go Rebels!" everyone responded.

I headed back to where the drill team was still gathered.

"Rodya. Good news. The members of the drill team have decided you pass inspection. We want you to be our mascot. Rod the Bod, surfer boy from Miami, Mascot of the Thomas Jefferson High School Drill Team."

"That's really neat. I'm honored. I wish I could come here with you next week and get to know everyone better. Too bad we have to leave tomorrow after the unveiling for our trip to Clarksville. Wish I went to T.J. High."

"Mascot of the drill team. Oh, the possibilities. Stevie Bagelman would be so jealous if he knew I was hanging out with the entire drill team," I thought.

Just then a boy walked up holding his trombone. Tall and thin, he had about a million freckles on his nose. His unruly reddish brown hair had a cowlick sticking up in the back. He looked a little bit like Archie Andrews and a little bit like Huckleberry Finn. "Hey, Suzy," he said, while carelessly emptying the trombone's spit valve.

"Oh, hey, Donny."

"You looked great out there in practice. I was wondering. Do you think you might like to go bowling with me some time?" he asked. His voice cracked as he rocked nervously back and forth.

"Sure, Donny. That'd be fun," said Suzy, trying to act nonchalant.

"That's swell, Suzy. I'll call you, and we'll go out. I can't wait." Donny gave Suzy his widest smile, revealing all his teeth, totally wired and glistening with new metal braces.

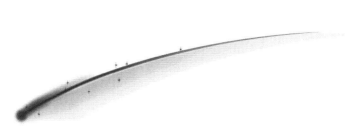

UNVEILING

THE HOUSE BEGAN to fill with guests returning from the cemetery. It had been one year since the funeral of Uncle Shuki, and today was the day his headstone was unveiled. The baby brother of Mom and her brothers and sister had a massive stroke at age thirty-four, out of the clear blue sky. Family and friends were still shocked and devastated by the loss.

Tables were covered with platters of food, including bagels and lox, whitefish, pickled herring, kugels, knishes, fruit salads, vegetable salads, and potato salads. Another table held desserts— mandelbroit, rugelach, cookies, and cakes. The alcohol began to flow, and the crowd grew louder and louder. Conversation and laughter filled the room. I wondered why people got so happy at such a sad occasion.

"Shah! Will everyone please quiet down! My brother is dead, and you're all laughing and carrying on like this is New Year's Eve." Uncle Will's voice carried over the din in the room. "Shuki died one year ago, and we must respect his memory. I spent a week sitting next to his bed at Parkland Memorial Hospital while he slipped away. The doctors could do nothing to bring him back from his coma. Every time I drive down Harry Hines Boulevard past that hospital, I feel so sad that tears come to my eyes. Parkland Memorial Hospital is the saddest place in the world. A great man died there. I'll never forget seeing my brother being removed from the ambulance and taken unconscious into the hospital emergency room. So have some respect for me and my brother, *oliv a shalom*, and let's have a solemn occasion in his memory."

The room grew still. The embarrassed guests got completely quiet. Within a few minutes, people began to whisper and talk quietly again. Aunt Betty approached me.

"Roddy, there are some people here who would like to meet you," she said.

She walked me over to a middle-aged couple. The man was tall and slim, with silver hair combed and parted in a pompadour. He was standing very straight and tall next to a short, pleasant-looking older woman who was slightly stooped and breathed with an audible sigh at the end of each exhale. There was a noticeable tremor in her hand, which grasped a gold-tipped cane. She had many lines on her face and a rather sad appearance. She looked at me with her deep blue eyes, and I thought they revealed the same kindness that I also had seen in my mother's and grand-mother's eyes.

"This is your mother's cousin Martha and her husband Thaddeus Mazurski. They asked to meet you," said Aunt Betty.

"This is Jenny's son and Tante Chava's grandson? Oh, Thaddy, look at him. He is the image of my poor brother Rueven, *oliv a shalom*," Martha said as she stroked my cheek.

"Yes. I see the resemblance," replied Thaddeus in a thick European accent. "Such a sweet-looking boy."

"Rueven? That's my Jewish name," I said. "What a coincidence that I have the same name as your brother."

"Thaddy, do you hear him? My brother and this young man were both named for my zaydeh, Rueven. There is another Rueven in the family. Perhaps now my brother's soul can rest in peace," she said as she covered her mouth with her hands.

"I met your lovely mama last year when she was here for your uncle's funeral. Jenny is a beautiful woman. She is my first cousin. Our mothers were sisters. Even though it was the first time we met, we felt like family immediately. She is sweet like our grand-mother. Jenny's mother, Tante Chava, was the prettiest girl in the village. Lively, sweet, and smart. No one in the village was a better dancer. At weddings and bar mitzvahs, when they played a Kazotchka, she kicked out her legs higher and faster than anyone. I was afraid she would fall, but she never did.

"How Mama and my grandmama missed Chavale when she left the *shtetl* and moved to America as a young girl. Why, oh why, didn't we all leave Europe? During the terrible days after the Nazis came, I dreamed of America and envied the lucky people who had left Poland. My prayers for their safety were answered. Why, oh why, didn't God listen to my prayers for the Jews of our village?

"How many children does your mother have? A large brood, as I recall," asked Martha as she ran her wrinkled hands over her lower abdomen.

"I have three sisters and a brother. My brother was born nine months after Grandma Eva died. Mom believes a soul doesn't rest peacefully until a new baby is born and is given the name of a dear departed person. Mom wanted Grandma's soul to rest in peace, so my brother was named Evan, after Chava's English name, Eva." I explained.

"Five children. That's wonderful. *Zayt gezunt*. Rueven, live and be well. Have many children and raise them to be good Jews," said Martha, as she clasped my hands in hers.

I looked down at her hands and noticed a series of numbers tattooed on her left forearm. I realized at once that my mother's cousin had been tattooed in a concentration camp. A survivor of the most horrible event in history was standing right in front of me.

✻ ✻ ✻

I went back to Suzy's bedroom where the other kids my age were hanging out.

"I see you met Thaddeus and Martha, Rod," said Suzy.

"Yes, what's the story with the tattoo on her arm?"

"Mom told me all about her. During World War II, the Nazis sent her and all the Jews in her village to Auschwitz concentration camp. They took her, her brothers and sisters, her parents, and all their aunts and uncles. They even took her grandparents, who were our great grandparents. Everyone was tattooed, herded like cattle to the gas chambers, and killed immediately, except for Martha. She stood out because she had blonde hair, blue eyes, and lovely features. She also had worked as a nurse. The Nazis decided not to kill her, but they did put that tattoo on her arm. They put her to work as a nurse in a hospital where non-Jews were treated.

"One day Thaddeus Mazurski, a Polish army officer, came into the hospital as a patient. Martha was serving as his nurse, and he was charmed by her. They fell in love. Non-Jews were not supposed to associate with Jews, and they certainly were not allowed to fall in love with them. Thaddeus was determined to find a way to free Martha from Auschwitz. Risking his own life, he bribed some Nazi guards. They agreed that she would be secretly released into Thad's custody. Before her release from the death camp, she was taken to a Nazi doctor. The Nazis wanted to be sure that Jewish women would not reproduce. She was taken to be sterilized. The torturers, who had been trained as doctors, performed a hysterectomy without using any anesthesia. Somehow she recovered from the operation and was one of the few Jews to leave Auschwitz alive. She and Thad managed to survive the rest of the war hiding with his friends on a remote farm in Poland. After the war ended, they married, decided to leave Europe, and came to live in Dallas. Martha was the only one of our Polish relatives that survived. How that woman has suffered. Mom says she and her Thaddy love each other very much."

"Wow!" I said. "A love story and a horror story combined. I've been reading about World War II, but I had no idea that our own cousins experienced so much horror. This is unforgettable. I don't think I'll be able to sleep tonight."

"Hey, do you guys smell the coffee? I'm starting to get hungry. Let's go munch on some of those yummy desserts," said Marilyn.

We moved back into the front of the house, where the guests had started to talk a little louder. Many of the adults had the glow of several drinks of liquor on their faces.

"Rodya, dahlink, would you pour me a cup of coffee?" asked Marilyn in a fake Russian accent.

"Sure. How do you like it?" I asked, while chewing on my third chocolate chip cookie.

"No cream and two sugars: black and sweet like my men," laughed Marilyn, speaking louder than she had intended.

Bursting into laughter and spitting out crumbs, I nearly choked on my cookie. Every adult in the room stared in Marilyn's direction. Many of them looked shocked at what they had heard my cute young cousin say.

"Marilyn, really," scolded Suzy.

"Oops, I did it again. Maybe someday I'll act more demure," laughed Marilyn, only slightly embarrassed.

Everyone in the room was still staring at Marilyn as Uncle Will spoke up again. Looking lovingly at his daughters, he gently scolded, "Children, please! Shah! Respect." In his eyes they would always be his darling little girls.

CHAPTER 11
THE HUB

I T WAS MY first day in Clarksville, Texas, at the home of my
Uncle Harry, Aunt Ruby, and my cousin, Mark Wise. We walked
downtown and entered the dry goods store that was the family
business of the Wise family.

"Welcome to the Hub. We're mighty proud of this store. Folks
come from parts of Oklahoma, Arkansas, Louisiana, and even as
far away as Dallas to shop here. It's not only that our prices are
the lowest, but everyone loves our friendly hometown service,"
said my Uncle Harry as we walked into his store.

The Hub was the most prominent structure on Clarksville's
rustic old town square. It was the only two-story building and
was topped by a large neon sign that had the name of the store
in script under the outline of a large ten-gallon hat. Many of the
other stores were vacant and boarded up. The modest commercial
center of Clarksville surrounded a small wooded park. There
were benches in front of a statue honoring Texas's Confederate
soldiers shaded by large trees. Even though there were no horses
or buggies clip clopping by, I felt like I was on the set of a western
movie.

Standing six feet two inches, Uncle Harry was the tallest
member of the Wise family. He was a handsome man and had
what could be described as a Roman nose. A slight bump on its
bridge gave just a hint of his Jewish heritage. He wore his wavy
brown hair combed straight back with perhaps just a little dab
of Brylcreem. His eyes were exactly the same shade of blue as my

mother's. When he smiled his welcoming grin, I noticed that his left front tooth slightly overlapped the right one. His black pants and short-sleeved white shirt were neatly pressed and spotless. He wore cowboy boots that were polished a spit-shined brown. His belt buckle glistened with a gold six-pointed star that looked like a sheriff's badge. It might also have served as a reminder that Uncle Harry was the only Jewish resident of Clarksville.

"To succeed around here, we have to be special because Clarksville is not a growing town anymore. Agriculture around here has taken a downturn, and the young people are moving out to live in the big cities where there are more opportunities. The buildings are getting a little dilapidated, but it's our home, and we love it," he continued.

As we entered the store, we were greeted by a red-haired, red-faced man who was obviously one of my uncle's employees. He was a short but muscular man who looked about twenty-five years old. His red hair was cut in a crew cut that was so short he might just as well have been bald.

"Howdy, Boss. It's sure enough busy in here today. We're packed with folks buying school clothes for their kids. Mostly the usual good local folks and even some city slickers all the way from Texarkana. I guess they're trying to avoid the big rush around Labor Day."

"Roddy, I want you to meet my employee. His family calls him Junior Boy, but we just call him J.B."

"J.B, this is my sister's oldest boy, Roddy. He's here visiting from Miami. He and my Mark are exactly the same age."

"Howdy, pardner. Welcome to the Hub. Feel free to take a look around the premises. You'll have to excuse me. I don't have time to give you the grand tour. There's plenty of work to do around here," said J.B., speaking in a slow nasal Texas drawl. "Boss, I'm goin' over yonder to help out Big Paul and Young Paul. Young Paul needs to get fit with some new duds. After that, I'll help Big Paul pick out some fabric to recover their old couches."

"It's a pleasure meeting you, J.B." I responded as he sized me up.

We shook hands. He grasped my hand and squeezed my fingers so hard it felt like they were going to break. After he released his grip, I had to rub the palm of my right hand with my left thumb to ease the pain. As he turned and walked away, I heard him whisper disdainfully, "Gawd damn city boy."

"That J.B. kind of reminds me of me when I was a young man—full of energy, ambitious, and not afraid to learn new things. He can fix nearly everything too. Not afraid to get his hands dirty. He's a great salesman with the locals. Speaks their language. If he seems a little rough around the edges, it's because he's just a country boy who has never traveled more than a hundred miles from Clarksville. It can take him a while to warm up to folks who aren't from around here," said Uncle Harry.

"I've been working at this store for over thirty years. I came to Texas from Ohio at age sixteen. I knew that I didn't want to end up working in the rubber factories of Akron, so I dropped out of school, said a tearful goodbye to my loving parents, and drove west to seek my fortune. I took a junked car and worked for months fixing it up and making it drivable. I named my old jalopy "Snoony". She had a rumble seat but no brakes. I downshifted and threw out the anchor when I wanted to stop.

"I had heard stories of fortunes being made by Texans striking it rich drilling for oil. Those oil fields bursting with black gold, "Texas tea", seemed to be calling to me. It was very exciting to cross the state line and drive into the Lone Star State. Clarksville was the first town I came to just after crossing the Red River into Texas. Being flat broke, I walked into the Hub and asked Old Man Clark for a job. He must have liked the cut of my jib because he hired me on the spot.

"My plan was to work a while and save enough money to continue on to the oil fields. I swept floors, lifted boxes, and even scrubbed the toilets. I was young, energetic and in constant motion. I always tried to please the customers and was very good at helping them find what they wanted. In no time flat, Mr. Clark made me a salesman and offered me a bonus if I met our goals. I don't mind saying, I was a right good salesman. I had a knack for knowing just how much of each item to buy and what merchandise wouldn't sell. Pretty soon Mr. Clark was taking me to market and letting me order the merchandise. We were able to keep our prices lower than anyone else in the four-states area. That's really the key to success in the retail business.

"The day Ruby walked into the Hub, I fell in love with her. We had a few dates and then decided to get hitched right away. Both of our families were shocked that we would marry someone from another religion, but we knew we could make it work. She's my one and only. I guess you could call us soul mates.

We settled into small town life as in love as two people could be. Before long, I was so content living in Clarksville with Ruby and working at the Hub, I completely stopped thinking about becoming an oilman.

"The Clarks didn't have any children to turn the store over to. As the years passed, they began to treat me like a son. When Mr. Clark decided it was time to retire, he offered to sell me the place. I had saved up some money and had a good reputation as a businessman. The bank lent me enough money to buy out the Clarks, and today I am the owner of the most successful retail store in Red River County."

We started walking down the aisles completely stocked with merchandise. Men's clothing, women's clothing, children's clothing, blankets, sheets, quilts, and bolts of multicolored and patterned fabric were piled high, almost reaching the ceiling. Halfway down one of the aisles, Uncle Harry stopped suddenly and grabbed my arm. He put his finger to his lips to hush me with an urgency that shocked me. I soon understood why. Coming from the next aisle, we could hear the conversation between two men speaking with distinctive and grating Texas drawls.

"It will be a real feather in my cap both in heaven and among my fellow pastors when I bring a converted Jew into the flock. Yes sir, a real feather in my cap. Imagine a Jew converting to become a member of our Clarksville Christian Church," said one voice.

"Yes. To bring a Jew to Christ is very difficult. They are a stubborn and stiff-necked people. I envy you. The Lord smiles down on one who saves the damned soul of a Jew. I wish I could get a Jew to convert to our Baptist church," replied the other voice.

"I don't know if Harry has truly opened his heart to the Lord. But I do know that he would do anything for his sweet wife Ruby. She has prayed and prayed that he would become a member of the Clarksville Christian Church, and it looks like now our prayers will be answered. I suspect he will join our congregation and step forward for Christ any Sunday now," stated the first voice proudly.

"You know, Harry's parents came to this country from Poland. His real name isn't Harry Wise. It's Herschel Veishaus. You know what happened to the Jews they left behind in the countries the Germans conquered. I sure wouldn't have wanted to be a Jew in Europe during World War II. The Nazis found them wherever they were hiding. Heh heh heh," laughed the Baptist minister.

"It's hard to understand why they didn't just all become Christians in Germany. They could have had salvation in the Lord and salvation from their Nazi persecutors," stated the first minister.

"No, no, McCracken, you're not clear on your history. It didn't work like that at all. Facing discrimination and death, some Jews tried to become Christians or denied they were Jews. In reality, the Nazis were seeking racial purity. For them the Jews were an inferior race, not just a religion that didn't recognize that the Messiah had been born. Even if you were a church member, if you had a Jewish parent or grandparent the Nazis would hunt you down, deport you to a concentration camp, and send you to the gas chamber," explained the Baptist minister.

"In any case, once Harry Wise is baptized, there'll be one less Jew and one more soul in the service of our Lord. Everyone will be better off. What I call a win-win situation," proclaimed the pastor of the Clarksville Christian Church.

Uncle Harry's face turned very red. I noticed him clenching and unclenching his fists and his brow furrowing with rage. He held his finger to his lips letting me know he wanted me to stay quiet. Placing his hand on my back, he guided me out the front door and onto the sidewalk in front of the Hub. Once outside his store, Uncle Harry whistled loudly and called out, "Here, Sputnik. Here, boy." A white hound with a black ring around one eye pranced over and jumped up on my uncle, who rewarded the dog by patting him on the head. "Good old Spooter. Good boy, Sputnik. Good dog."

Sputnik jumped up on me, and I started petting him. He licked my face before running back to Uncle Harry. On Sputnik's side was a large area where no hair was growing. His exposed skin was inflamed and raw.

"What happened to your dog? Why does Sputnik have a bald spot?" I asked.

"A few weeks ago Sputnik came crawling home whimpering. His skin was still smoking. Someone had thrown acid on him. I have no idea why. Sputnik never hurt a soul. He doesn't even bark much. Why would anyone intentionally hurt my sweet dog? I hope they didn't attack my dog trying to get at me. Poor pup suffered for days with that burn. You're okay now, aren't you boy? Good dog. Good old Spooter."

Uncle Harry, Sputnik and I walked slowly back to Uncle Harry and Aunt Ruby's house.

"I'm sure Ruby and Myrlie will have a wonderful dinner ready for us. I hope you're hungry. I seemed to have lost my appetite," said Uncle Harry shaking his head and pursing his lips together tightly.

We turned the corner and approached a church. "This is the Clarksville Christian Church. I will never set foot in it again," said Uncle Harry, as he cleared his throat of phlegm and saliva and spat it bitterly on the step leading to the front door of the church.

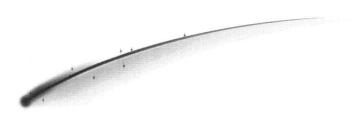

CHAPTER 12
BACK ROADS

"PLEASE, UNCLE HARRY, please, please, puhleeeze let me drive your car. I'm a great driver. Right, Roddy?" begged Marilyn.

Wanting to stay on Marilyn's good side and excited to go for a drive in the Bonneville, I weighed in, "I'd have to say I'm impressed. She was very smooth driving me around Dallas. She works the clutch and shifts gears like an old pro. She obeys the traffic rules at all times, too."

"We'll just drive down to the lake. I won't speed. I'll be very careful. I just love your new car, Uncle Harrykins."

"Have I ever said no to you, sweetheart? You've always had me wrapped around your little finger. Stop batting your eyes at me. Okay, sweet sixteen, you can drive my brand new car, but remember it's my pride and joy," Uncle Harry reluctantly conceded. I was a little surprised to see him cave in so easily to Marilyn.

Throwing her arms around him, Marilyn kissed him on the cheek and thanked her uncle repeatedly. "You're my best guy. I'll love you til the end of time. I promise we won't be gone long. We'll be back in an hour. Come on, let's go, Markles, you pokey puppy."

"No thanks," said Mark. "It must be 105 degrees today. I don't need to drive around Clarksville. I'd rather stay home and drink some of Myrlie's sweet iced tea. Be careful, Marilyn. Next year I get my restricted, and I don't want any scratches on my ride."

Bowing deeply Marilyn replied, "All righty then, let's go cruising without Emperor Marcus Aurelius, the next owner of this beautiful chariot."

"Shotgun."

"Stuck in the backseat as usual," complained Suzy.

We climbed into Uncle Harry's shiny new white Bonneville with blue leather interior.

"Can I put the top down? I've never been in a convertible before. I can't wait to feel the wind in my hair," cooed Marilyn, using her flirtiest voice.

Uncle Harry reached through the window and pulled the lever that caused the convertible roof to retract. Marilyn grabbed his arm and squeezed his bicep in admiration.

"Have fun, kids. Marilyn, promise me, no speeding. Remember, one hour. I'll be waiting and checking my watch."

Marilyn turned the key, revved the motor, and kicked up a few pebbles as she drove away from the house. We made a left turn on Main Street, drove past Clarksville High School, and headed out of town on U.S. 82.

"Wow. Automatic transmission. My first time not having to use the clutch. This is so easy to drive compared to the old Galaxy. Rides smooth as silk. With the top down and the wind blowing, you'd never know it's over 100 degrees today. Let's check out this radio."

Marilyn started going through the preset radio stations on the dashboard. Country music blared out of each station. "I can't believe Uncle Harry likes this hillbilly music. Roddy, see if you can find a station playing real rock and roll for the young folks who live out here in the boondocks."

I started turning the radio dial, but all I got was static and an occasional distorted voice. At the very top of the dial some faint music could be heard.

"Oh, wow, tune that in. Sounds like rock and roll," commanded Marilyn.

I moved the dial back and forth until the sounds of the Surfaris' "Wipe Out" could be clearly heard. Back in Miami, our high school marching band always used the long drum solo from "Wipe Out" as a football cheer. While the drummers played "Wipe Out", the fans all chanted "Go, go, go, go, go...go!" as we anticipated a kickoff. Like every other young guy I knew, I practiced it constantly on any hard surface I could find to drum on. Now I pounded out the drum solo on the dashboard while Suzy drummed along against the back of my seat.

"This is Big Dan Ingram bringing you the best rock 'n' roll tunes here in North Texas. 1480 on your radio dial."

"Yeah, yeah! It's KBOX all the way from Dallas. There's hope for teenagers in Clarksville after all," said Marilyn as she cranked up the volume until the speakers started rattling.

Soon we were singing the next song Big Dan played. We belted out Nat King Cole's celebration of the lazy hazy crazy summer days at the top of our lungs. I tried to imitate his deep, mellow voice. I sure wish I could have sung like Nat at my bar mitzvah. I'm sure Helen Christofilaki would have been very impressed.

Suzy kept drumming on the back of my seat. I could feel the beat from head to toe. We were a few miles outside of Clarksville, and it looked like we were the only car on the highway.

"Come on, Marilyn," I said. "Let's see what this Bonneville can do. My ass is draggin'."

Marilyn eased down on the gas pedal and accelerated past 60 miles per hour. We were now officially breaking the speed limit and still accelerating. In a few seconds we were rolling along at 70.

"You think this car will go a hundred?" Marilyn asked, as she floored the gas pedal.

"Marilyn, slow down. You promised Uncle Harry you'd be careful. You're going too fast," Suzy shouted from the backseat.

Marilyn was deaf to Suzy's pleas. She was ecstatic, racing down the highway. With the wind blowing through her hair, she reached down to crank up the volume on the radio as Skeeter Davis's song "End of the World" came on. I thought maybe the song was a prophecy, like the soundtrack to some tragic movie. Suddenly, a flock of birds flew across the road right in front of us. Marilyn, clearly startled by the sight of the birds and distracted by the radio, began to lose control of the car. The car swerved violently as she slammed on the brakes. She grabbed the wheel, and I grabbed the seat. Suzy screamed. A vision of the car rolling over and over before crashing into a tree flashed through my mind. "This really is the end of the world," I said to myself. Somehow Marilyn managed to gain control of the car and keep us on the road. Shaken and sobered and breathing a huge sigh of relief, she slowed us down to way below the speed limit.

"Okay, Suzy, you pooty parper. You're right. I shouldn't have been driving so fast. Besides, the wind is turning my hair into a ridiculous tangled mess. Anyway, I think it's time to do some exploring," said Marilyn trying to act like nothing had happened. "Let's get off this main road and check out the countryside. Maybe we'll find some excitement," she said as she turned down a narrow road leading into the woods.

"Marilyn, I'm not so sure this is a good idea," warned the ever-cautious Suzy.

"No, let's drive down this road a little while. I crave some adventure," I said, as the car began to kick up some dust and gravel began to clink against the underside of the car.

The road got narrower and narrower. Thick vines coated the pine trees. We passed a few isolated houses with overgrown gardens and broken-down wooden fences. Suzy waved to an old man sitting on his front porch in a rocking chair, smoking a corncob pipe.

"Ugh, he's got an outhouse. There's even a little moon on the door. Look at the curly tails on those little piglets penned up in his backyard. A billy goat is grazing on the dandelions. We really are in the boonies," said Suzy.

Marilyn turned down an even narrower dirt road. Gravel and rocks banged hard against the factory paint of the Bonneville.

"I wonder who could possibly live way out here?" she said. "This is starting to make me nervous. It's time to head back to Uncle Harry's. We're already late."

There wasn't any place to turn around as the woods came right up to the road. Marilyn was driving very slowly. The potholes in the road resembled the craters on the moon. We could hardly see because the car was kicking up so much dust. Finally, we came to a rusty barbed wire barrier with a sign that said "Keep Out".

"I guess they mean us," Marilyn said, as she stopped and threw the car into reverse. "It's going to be tough backing up all the way to that other road. I think I'll try to turn around. Rod, turn that blasted radio off right now. It's distracting me." Marilyn inched the car back until the rear wheels were off the road and into the bushes at the edge of the woods. "Rod, Suzy, watch behind the car for me. I don't want to hit a tree."

Blam! The car lurched backward and stopped suddenly. The back wheels had fallen into a small ditch about two feet deep. Marilyn put the car back into drive and tried to drive forward. The tires just spun and kicked up a huge amount of dust that began to settle on the Bonneville's pristine new blue upholstery.

"Crap. I didn't see that ditch. It must have been covered up by leaves and branches. Uncle Harry is gonna kill me."

"Try going forward and backward and see if you can get the tires to catch," I suggested.

She did what I said but the car only moved slightly, and as the wheels spun and spun, I began to smell burning rubber and oil. The upholstery and all of us sitting in the stuck car became covered in dust and dirt.

"Come on. Get out and push, you guys. Use all your strength," Marilyn begged, clearly losing her composure.

Suzy and I got behind the car and pushed with all our might. We might as well have been trying to lift a Brahma bull. The car was going nowhere.

"Looks like we have to walk back to that farmer's house and see if he can help us. Did you see a tractor back there?" said Marilyn, barely holding back tears.

"Marilyn, I told you not to drive off the main highway. We told Uncle Harry we were going to the lake and would be back in an hour. It's already been an hour and half."

"Shut up, Suzy, and walk."

We started walking, and immediately the gnats began buzzing around us, and the mosquitoes started biting. My shirt was soaked with sweat.

"It must be over 100 degrees. It's burning hot, like that song 'Heat Wave' on the radio. It's not burning in my heart. It's burning my feet," I complained.

"Pipe down, bonehead. You're no Martha Reeves," scolded Marilyn.

We trudged on in silence with our anxiety growing.

"Oh my God, look at that spider web," cried Suzy.

Just off the side of the road, a gigantic spider web stretched at least ten feet between two trees. Dozens of bugs were caught up in it, some still squirming.

"I think I'm in a bigger fix than those bugs caught in that enormous web," whimpered Marilyn.

"What is that thing, a tarantula? That is one Texas-sized spider," I marveled. "Do you think there might be wolves or bobcats around here?"

Marilyn started to chant, "Lions and tigers and bears, oh my. Lions and tigers and bears, oh my." Suzy and I chanted with her as we trudged along in rhythm.

"I'm thirsty, and I have to pee. This is getting ridiculous," said Suzy. "There are mosquitoes buzzing around me. I'm sweating. We've walked miles."

Finally, exhausted and frustrated, we arrived at the small ramshackle house we had driven by a few hours ago. I looked over at the girls and observed that they were so soaked in sweat that their clothes stuck to their bodies like snake skins ready to be shed.

"Look! There's the house. I'm sure that old man can help us," said Marilyn, hopefully.

"Howdy, young'uns," he greeted us. Limping down the rotting wooden steps of his creaky porch, he said, "I saw you drive by here. Knew you'd be back. My name's Johnson Creech. Where's that fine-looking automobile you were driving?"

"Marilyn drove us into a ditch. Can I have a glass of water? I need to use the lady's room, too," moaned Suzy.

"Got no plumbing or electricity out here. Come on in the house and fill up a jar with some water from my drinkin' bucket, unless you prefer a little moonshine. Here, take a pull out of this here jug. I'm always lookin' for a drinkin' partner. It burns goin' down, but it feels good when it hits your belly. Over yonder's the shithouse, young lady. It's not like what you're used to."

"Just some water please. It's so hot today," said Marilyn, refusing the jug that he tried to pass her.

Suzy walked back to the outhouse, while Marilyn and I sipped water from semi-clean mason jars. We tried to ignore the little specks floating in the water. They looked harmless and didn't seem to be moving around like they were alive.

"Mr. Creech, do you think you could help us pull Uncle Harry's car out of the ditch? It's just the back tires. We can't get it to budge," I asked.

"Sure enough, my tractor will pull you right out. Where did I put those keys?" he said as he moved things around on the kitchen counter that was covered with dirty dishes, old food wrappers, and partially opened cans of dog food. I wondered who was eating the dog food, Mr. Creech or his dogs? "Here they are. They must have fell off the key hook where I left them a few days ago. My memory's not what it used to be."

As he bent over to pick up his keys, his unbelted old jeans drooped, exposing the top of his butt crack. This was a sight for no one's eyes.

Suzy walked back into the room, her face a little green. "That was disgusting. What a smell. Next time I'll hide behind a tree. It's more sanitary. I wish I was a boy."

We walked back onto the porch. Nailed to a wooden post was a large, round, rusty thermometer advertising Coca-Cola. The temperature dial pointed to 106 degrees. We walked back down the creaky porch steps. One of the boards popped loose as I stepped on it. I fell through it and scraped my shin.

"Careful now. Been meaning to fix that for a long time."

Johnson Creech mounted the tractor with a leer on his face. His face was covered with several days' growth of stubbly gray and white whiskers. He stared at the girls' underwear, visible through their sweat-soaked clothes. "There's room for one more on this tractor. I'll drive slow so the other two can keep up with us. Why don't one of you two fine young cherries climb up here next to me?" He reached his hands down to help one of my cousins board his tractor. Repulsed, Suzy and Marilyn abruptly turned away from him and got behind the tractor. It was obvious they preferred to walk than sit near the old redneck. I climbed aboard the tractor and sat down. We rolled slowly down the dirt road as the girls walked a few steps behind us. Unable to resist teasing them, I starting singing the Four Seasons' hit "Walk Like a Man".

"Shut up!" they screamed at the same time.

"We're not walking like a man, and we're not your sons," scolded the tired and frustrated Marilyn.

When we finally got back to the car, the grizzled old geezer crawled under the car and found a place to tie a rope to the frame of the car. Then he attached the rope to the rear of his tractor.

"Don't have a proper tow line, but this ought to work. Make sure your car's in neutral."

He restarted the tractor and began to move forward, but the Bonneville wouldn't budge. After several tries, he said, "No luck. That's one heavy car. Is your Uncle Harry, Mayor Harry Wise, owner of the Hub?"

"Yes, that's him. He's going to kill me," said Marilyn.

"He's a mighty fine man. Treats everyone fair. He gives me credit at the Hub when I'm short on cash. I always tell that J.B. who works for Harry, 'Don't believe that stuff folks say about Jews and money. Harry is a Jew, but he's the finest, most generous man I know.'" Creech continued, "Y'all should be ashamed of yourself for what you done to this fine automobile. Stay right here and I'll drive up yonder to the phone booth back on the main road and let Harry know everything that's going on out here."

An hour passed like an eternity as Marilyn, Suzy and I speculated about what Uncle Harry was going to do to us.

uzy and I are going back to Dallas tomorrow. Uncle Harry and Aunt Ruby will never let us come visit them again. Goodbye forever, Clarksville," Marilyn cried, with a tear running down her cheek.

Finally, we heard the sound of tires against the dirt road. It was J.B. and Johnson Creech in Grandpa's ancient Studebaker. Seeing Grandpa's Wise's old car brought back memories of my mother's sweet father, and the year he lived with us before he died. It was in that Studebaker that I had my very first disaster in a car. I was about four years old. Grandpa had been packing up the Studebaker for a trip to Florida. I was curious and wanted to help him load the car. He cautioned me, "I'm busy now. Stay away from the car. Something bad might happen to you." Just an instant later, he accidently closed the car door on my thumb. I howled in pain. My thumb was swollen and bruised for a month. How had Grandpa known that I was going to get hurt? I still missed my gentle grandfather. After Grandpa died, Uncle Harry inherited his car. I was surprised to see that it was still running. Jumping out of the slightly rusted and dented Studebaker, J.B. scolded, "Look at the mess you kids made. I dropped Harry off at the mechanic's place. He'll be waiting for you, and I have to tell you, he is not happy. If I was your uncle, I'd tan your hides."

Mustering the last of my sense of humor, I couldn't resist singing a line from "Tie Me Kangaroo Down, Sport", about that poor Australian, Clyde, who died and then got his hide tanned and hung on the shed. Despite the miserable situation, the girls both burst out laughing.

"Watch it, Rodger Dodger, or I'll whip you myself," threatened J.B.

"Now watch a real Texan in action. Marilyn, get behind the wheel. Suzy and Hot Rod, get in the car." J.B attached a tow bar from the Studebaker to the Bonneville and slowly drove forward. The rear wheels of the Bonneville rolled forward and right up out of the ditch.

"Yabba dabba doo!" I shouted.

"Hush up, Boo Boo Bear. Y'all are in big trouble. I'm going to tow you to your uncle's mechanic. Marilyn, be ready to brake when I slow down so you don't crash these two cars together."

"Doesn't he mean Yogi Bear?" whispered Suzy in my ear.

"Fred Flintstone," I laughed very quietly.

"Creech, I'll drop you off back at your shack. Have you thought about what we discussed at our last meeting over in Bug Tussle?" asked J.B.

"Count me out, J.B. I'm too old and tired for that kind of business. Some of them boys you been hanging out with are dumber than jackasses. Maybe y'all better just settle down and stay out of trouble. Things ain't never gonna be like they was in the old days. It might be hard for you to understand it now, but there's good and bad in all people. T'ain't no need for anyone to get hurt," replied Johnson Creech.

We dropped Mr. Creech off at his house. As he climbed the steps, he turned back to J.B. and said, "Don't want no young ones to get hurt. Mind what I say, J.B." Then he winked at Marilyn and Suzy and said, "Gals, y'all come back now."

A few minutes later we were at the gas station where Uncle Harry was waiting with his hands on his hips and his right foot tapping the floor anxiously. The car was filthy inside and out. Uncle Harry, while visibly relieved to see us safe, was seething.

"Land's sake, Marilyn. You promised you would just drive to the lake. I was worried sick. I trusted you with my brand new car."

"I'm sorry, I'm sorry, I'm sorry. I learned my lesson. Can you ever forgive me?" she begged.

Uncle Harry patted her on the back and massaged her shoulders for a second, while shaking his head from side to side.

"I swan," was the worst curse he could muster.

After several minutes the mechanic finished checking out the car. "You'll be needing two new rear tires and all the oil has been burned up. I think she'll be almost good as new once we wash her down. I'm afraid that upholstery will never be the same, though."

"Fine, take care of it will you?" Uncle Harry sighed. "You kids are a mess. Thank God you're safe. You must be starving. I'll drop you off for steak dinners at my favorite restaurant, The Alps."

We drove to the restaurant and Uncle Harry walked in with us. Tables and booths were covered with white tablecloths. The head of a buck with huge antlers was centered over the brick fireplace.

There were steaks sizzling on the grill visible in the kitchen. The aroma of sautéed onions and garlic made my mouth water.

"Hi, Sally," he said in his friendly way to the waitress. "These kids are hungry. I hope you can grill some Texas-raised filet mignons for them. I love it when the steaks are wrapped in bacon. Make sure you load those baked potatoes with plenty of butter and sour cream."

"Sure enough, Harry." The waitress looked at Marilyn and asked, "You the little girl who drove your uncle's new car into the ditch?"

"Word sure travels fast in this neck of the woods, doesn't it, kids? By tomorrow you'll be the talk of the town," said Uncle Harry. "I'm going to walk home and cool off a little. You kids have a big slice of chocolate cake for dessert and tell Sally to charge it to Harry Wise."

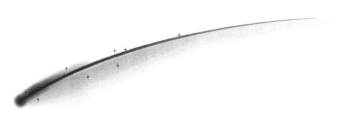

CHURCH SERVICE

Praise god, from whom all blessings flow;
Praise him, all creatures here below;
Praise him above, ye heavenly host;
Praise father, son, and holy ghost.

A S THE PREACHER of the Clarksville Christian Church led us in the doxology, I realized this was the first time I'd ever been inside a church.

We sat on the hard benches in the front row. The preacher led us in a hymn. Aunt Ruby and her sister Violet's voices were sweet and vibrant. They could be heard clearly over the singing of the entire congregation. Mark sang quietly and completely off key, while I, despite my bar mitzvah vows, attempted to join in the beautiful song of praise to the Christian trinity. "Now please read with me in unison from Mark 12:30. 'And you shall love the Lord your God with all your heart, and with all your soul, and with all your mind, and with all your strength: This is the first commandment.'"

Ah. This sounded familiar. The English translation of the V'ahavtah. I had been forced to memorize it in Hebrew and English along with my entire Hebrew school class. This was the prayer from the Old Testament Book of Deuteronomy commanding the Jews to love God and place a mezuzah at their front door. How comforting it was to hear Christians reading this important Jewish prayer. Maybe our religions weren't that different after all.

The service continued not completely unlike Friday night services at our shul in Miami. The preacher read a verse from the Bible. There was a responsive reading of a psalm. Songs were sung praising God. Aunt Ruby's strong voice rang out. We stood up and sat down as directed by the preacher. We read from our prayer books. How odd that Aunt Ruby licked her index finger right before she turned each page exactly as my grandmother did in synagogue. I found it interesting that the women wore hats in church while the men took theirs off. This was the opposite of the way things were at Beth Ami. In a synagogue, men always wore *kippot* on their heads to show humility before God.

Usually I quickly became bored at religious services, fidgeted, and fought the urge to doze off. Since I was sitting in the front row, I couldn't occupy myself by looking to see if there were any cute girls in the room. I studied the image of the crucified Jesus hanging on the front wall of the church sanctuary. These people believed this tortured, emaciated man was the son of God. As a Jewish man, I was not allowed to entertain such thoughts. The preacher spoke again, beginning his sermon.

"In John 14:6 Jesus told his disciples, 'I am the way and the truth and the life. No one comes to the Father except through me.'"

I thought he was looking directly at me as he explained this passage.

"Jesus Christ, the creator of all things, told a Jewish ruler that if he was not born again, then he would never see the Kingdom of God! The Jews claim to be the chosen people of God. The true Book of Life lies within the body of Christ. Unless you have faith in your salvation through Jesus Christ, you will burn in the fiery furnace of hell for all eternity. Of this there can be no doubt."

Beth Ami this was not. The preacher seemed like he was talking directly to me. I fervently wished he would look at someone else, but it was to no avail.

The preacher continued, and now he was shouting and throwing his hands into the air.

"Jesus came to seek and to save the lost, and his own people, the Jewish people, rejected him because they would not have Jesus reign over them. Jesus Christ was slain upon the cross for our sins. You are either in or you are out! If you are a Buddhist, Hindu, Muslim, or Jew you must be saved. Repent or be damned and burn in the fires of hell forever! Now believe me, these are not my words, and this is not my will—this is God's Word and God's Will. Woe be it unto me if I don't declare God's truth!"

This was making me nervous. Did he preach about the damnation of the Jews every week? Of course I didn't want to go to hell. Now the preacher made eye contact directly with me.

"If there are any here among us today who have not accepted Jesus as their savior, I beg you to come to the front of the church and be saved right this minute. Come, just as you are and be embraced by the love of the Lord and the love of this congregation. Amen."

"Amen," responded the congregation.

Sweat started to form on my upper lip. My heart began racing. There was no way I was going to walk to the front of the room and be a feather in this guy's cap. Pressure to accept Jesus as my savior was being applied by everyone in the room. Aunt Ruby, sensing my unease, reached over and covered my hand with hers. With understanding and affection she gave my hand a gentle squeeze. I sat firmly in my seat as the sermon ended. The moment passed, and I took a deep breath and relaxed a little bit.

The preacher continued, "And now, brothers and sisters in the Lord, we will celebrate the Eucharist. Our deacons will pass among you so that you can partake in the body and blood of Christ. This food we call the Holy Communion. No one is allowed to partake except those who believes that all the things we teach are true."

The deacons began to move throughout the congregation offering little paper cups with wine and small wafers that looked like matzoh. Aunt Ruby, Violet, and Mark all took cups and drank from them and ate their bread. The deacon offered me the bread and wine and said, "The body and blood of Christ."

I hesitated for a moment and then ate the wafer and drank the wine. It tasted like Tam Tams and grape juice.

"The Lord is with you, brother," the deacon said.

"Am I still a Jew?" I thought. "Have I betrayed my Jewish ancestors and my Hebrew school teachers? What will Grandpa Noodleman think?" No, I decided. I just had a little cracker and some juice, though I did feel a sense of approval from all the people sitting around me.

"Before I give the benediction I have a few announcements to make. For you young people, Sunday school will start a half hour after this service is over. For the entire congregation, there will be a church picnic next Sunday at five o'clock out at the old church campgrounds. Everyone is welcome to join in good food and fellowship. Please bring your friends and family."

The preacher then held his hands out in front of him and gave the benediction. "Now may the God of peace himself sanctify you completely, and may your whole spirit, soul, and body be preserved blameless at the coming of our Lord Jesus Christ. Amen."

"Amen," responded the worshipers.

The congregation slowly filed out of the church. Standing in front of the church, the preacher greeted the congregants and shook everyone's hand. "Nice to see you. Have a blessed week. Please tell your mother I'm praying for her. May the Lord help her recover from her ailment."

As we approached him I noticed the minister was standing right on the spot that Uncle Harry had cursed with his spit.

"Nice to see you, Ruby. I expected your fine husband would be joining us today. Is he under the weather? I pray he's well. I purchased some new boots at the Hub this week and am verily pleased with them."

"Lovely service as usual, Pastor McCracken. This is Harry's sister's boy, Rodger. He's visiting us from Miami. He and my Mark are becoming very good friends."

"Are you the little boy who drove your uncle's car into the ditch? I hear you had quite an adventure with those two cousins of yours from Dallas. I hope you'll join Mark at Sunday school this morning. I'm sure the other youngsters will be pleased to meet you."

"He'll be there, Pastor. See you at Wednesday prayer group, as always."

CHAPTER 14
SUNDAY SCHOOL

MARK LED ME into the small room where Sunday school class was held. About a dozen eighth and ninth graders were standing around waiting for the teacher to arrive. Almost immediately the guys gathered around Mark, who was half a head taller than every other boy in the class. Nearly six feet tall and letting his crew cut grow out, my cousin was the obvious leader of the pack. "Hey Mark, is this your cousin who drove your dad's new Bonneville convertible into the ditch?" asked one of the boys.

"Yes, Chris, this is Rod. He was in the car with Marilyn and Suzy, my cousins from Dallas. Marilyn was driving the car, but she says he egged her on. He was looking for adventure here in the excitement capital of the world, Clarksville, Texas."

"Excitement capital, that's a laugh. Nothing ever happens around here. We get our biggest thrills when they turn our bull calves into steers. Maybe someday a tornado will come and blow this place away," said Chris with all the sarcasm he could muster. A lovely looking girl with a clear complexion and a long brown ponytail looked at me and said in a lilting voice, "Hi there, Mark. I hear your cousin's from Florida. Is he a surfer?"

"Gayla, uh, hey. Sure he is. He's from Surf City, U.S.A. You know, *'Two girls for every boy,'*" answered Mark, singing every note out of tune.

"If I had a cousin from Florida, we'd be spending the summer at the beach. I'd be wearing my teeny weenie bikini and getting a tan all over my body. So would you, wouldn't you, Alice Lee?

Why would anybody want to leave paradise for this hick town?" asked Gayla.

"Okay class, please take your seats. No talking. Gayla and Alice Lee, spit out that gum. And I've told you both many times that all that eye makeup is sinful. Good Christian girls do not paint their faces like harlots."

Two girls, both wearing glasses and necklaces with silver crosses, were the only students who sat down. The rest of the class continued to stand around and chat. Gayla turned her back to the teacher and wiggled her extended middle finger so that her redheaded friend could see it. Her friend laughed and then stuck out her tongue. I could tell there were more spirits in this room than just the Holy Spirit.

"Take your seats please and stop acting like first graders. We have a test today. Do you all remember last week's assignment? Everyone should have the names of all the books of the New Testament memorized. You will each recite them in order."

Groaning, the kids slowly began to move toward their seats. I squeezed into my chair and noticed that students had carved their initials in the top of the wooden desk. Some initials were placed inside of crudely carved hearts. There was a hole in the upper-right-hand corner of the desk that was once used for an inkwell. No one paid much attention to the teacher and everyone looked like they had someplace else they'd rather be. This was obviously a teacher no one was afraid of. I might just as well have been in Sunday school class at Temple Beth Ami.

"Chris, please sit up straight. Johnny Jones, get your feet out of the aisle. Gayla Purdy, for the second and last time, stop chomping on that gum. You remind me of a cow chewing her cud. Alice Lee, put away that mirror and comb. I see we have a visitor to our class today. Mark, will you please introduce your guest to the class?"

"This is my cousin Rod, from Miami," muttered Mark.

"It's so nice of you to join us, Rod. I am Miss Agnes Moon. M. O. O. N. I heard about your adventure with your uncle's car. Praise the Lord that no one was hurt and that you were able to be pulled from the ravine you drove into. Now, I'm sure at your church you've been required to learn the names of all the books of the Bible. Would you like to stand and recite them for us?"

My face felt warm like all the blood was rushing to my cheeks. I didn't respond to her, but squirmed a little in my seat.

"You do go to Sunday school, don't you?"

"Yeah" I responded.

"Yeah?" she repeated sounding annoyed.

"Yes, I mean."

"Yes, what?" she asked in a clipped voice.

"Yes, I go to Sunday school."

"Don't you mean yes, ma'am?" she scolded.

"Huh?"

"Haven't you been taught that when an adult speaks to a child, the polite way to respond is 'yes ma'am' or 'no ma'am'?"

"No, ma'am."

The class burst out in laughter. Mark slapped his forehead then put his head down on his desk, unsuccessfully trying to conceal his laughter.

"Very well. Gayla please stand and recite all the books of the New Testament in order."

I was relieved that the attention of the teacher and class was no longer focused on me. All eyes turned to the lovely Gayla, who stood up then leaned against her desk still chewing away on her gum.

"Uh...uh...Matthew, Mark, Luke, John, Nuderonomy, Galoshes, Dalmations, First Peter, Second Peter. Peter Peter pumpkin eater," she sang with a wicked and knowing grin.

"Gayla, sit down right this instant. What am I going to do with you?"

"I know what I'd like to do with her," whispered Chris, loud enough for everyone to hear.

One of the girls wearing a necklace with the silver cross waved her hand high over her head.

"Amanda Huggins. Please recite the books of the New Testament loudly and clearly so that all your good Christian friends can hear you."

Amanda stood up. Her flowery dress reached down to her ankles. She was very skinny and appeared to still be completely flat chested. The pimples on her face were swollen and red. She had obviously been anxiously picking at them.

"Matthew, Mark, Luke, John, Acts, Romans, First Corinthians, Second Corinthians, Galatians, Ephesians, Philippians, Colossians, First Thessalonians, Second Thessalonians, First Timothy, Second Timothy, Titus, Philemon, Hebrews, James, First Peter, Second Peter, First John, Second John, Third John, Jude, and Revelation." Amanda recited the books precisely and with great confidence.

"Lovely, lovely, lovely. A-plus-plus-plus. You are setting a fine example for your classmates. You may return to your seat, Amanda."

"Thank you, ma'am," said Amanda as she sat down and lowered her eyes.

"Is there anyone else who is prepared to recite? I assigned this memorization last week."

No one responded. It was obvious that Amanda Huggins was the only student who had done her homework. Mrs. Moon picked up the rectangular eraser and cleaned the blackboard leaving white streaks in a curved horizontal pattern. She coughed slightly as she inhaled the white chalk dust that lingered in the air. The teacher picked up a piece of white chalk and began writing the 27 books of New Testament on the blackboard. When the chalk squeaked against the blackboard, we all winced at the sound that made my skin crawl. Miss Moon turned back to the class, leaning her back against the blackboard and said, "I am looking for another volunteer to recite the books of the New Testament. This is your chance to receive an A." She turned back toward the board and continued writing. She now had two large white chalk spots on the back of her skirt. Each chalk mark was centered on one of her butt cheeks.

One of the boys yelled out, "Butt...butt...butt, Miss Moon, we need more time to memorize all those Bible books. More time is all I'm ass-skin for."

Miss Moon turned back to writing on the blackboard as the boys in the class guffawed and laughed, showing their bravado and disdain for Miss Moon.

The same boy wadded up a piece of paper, chewed it up like a wad of tobacco, and sent it flying directly at Amanda. It hit her smack on the side of her face, and she shrieked.

"Leave me alone, Johnny Jones! Miss Moon, Miss Moooon..."

"Johnny Jones, go directly to Reverend McCracken's office and tell him that you threw a spit wad at Amanda Huggins, my best student. I'm sure the Reverend will be informing your parents about your un-Christian behavior."

Johnny got up and lumbered out of the room as one of the other boys mocked him, saying, "Johnny's going to get his ass whipped by Cracken and by his dad. Does your daddy still whip you with his switch out in the shed behind the silo?" His mocking laugh was designed to rub salt in the wound.

Johnny turned backed toward him and said, "Watch out, you jerk, or I'll turn you into a steer." Then, hands in his pockets, he slouched out the classroom door.

The clock on the wall, covered with dried spit wads, made a loud click as the minute hand ticked to the straight down position. It was 12:30, and the students began to stand up and walk out of the room.

"Class is not over until I say class is dismissed. Students, please return to your seats." Ignoring the teacher, everyone continued toward the door.

"Next week your assignment is to memorize the books of the New Testament in order. I hope you'll all be attending Wednesday prayer meeting. Class dismissed," Miss Moon said hastily.

As we walked out of the building I glanced over at Gayla who was whispering to her red-headed friend, Alice Lee. Our eyes met for a second, and I gave her my most winning smile. Gayla raised her eyebrows and then turned away from me. As she walked away, her ponytail moved side to side as did her rear end. I wasn't sure if she swung her hips for me to notice what a shapely tush she had or if she just walked that way naturally.

An older boy yelled out, "I sure wish my back porch had a swing like that."

I turned to Mark. "That Gayla is a fox. I'd sure like to get to know her."

Mark replied, "Gayla and I are neighbors. We've been in the same class since kindergarten. We used to play together all the time. She even wanted to play 'doctor' when we were little. Then, in fifth grade, her boobs sprouted. She stopped talking to me and all the other guys our age. I hear she and Alice Lee have been going out with some tough dudes from over in Oklahoma who ride broncs in the rodeo. Everyone knows she isn't a virgin anymore."

"Not a virgin? Wow. Do you think she'll be at that church picnic?"

Mark replied with great certainty, "She probably will be, but you have absolutely no chance."

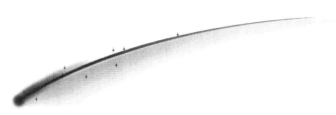

CHAPTER 15
SUNDAY DINNER

"**B**LESS US, OH Lord and these thy gifts which we are about to receive through thy bounty, through Christ Our Lord, Amen." Aunt Ruby unclasped my hand as she finished the blessing over our Sunday dinner.

"Ruby, you've outdone yourself," said Uncle Harry. "Rod, have you ever seen so much delicious food on one table?"

"Aunt Ruby, this looks and smells wonderful. Thank you so much for having me as a guest in your home," I said as a plate of crispy fried chicken was passed to me. There was fried chicken, fried okra, french fries, corn on the cob, green beans, coleslaw, cornbread, biscuits covered in butter, and to top it off, thinly sliced ham covered with pineapple. We all filled our plates and dug in for a feast.

"Harry, dear, don't fill up on the chicken and french fries. You know the doctor wants you to lower your cholesterol. I know how much your appetite has increased since you stopped smoking, but I'm so worried about your health." Said Aunt Ruby.

"Maybe I'll skip dessert," replied Uncle Harry as he bit into a drumstick and wiped his chin with a beautiful embroidered cloth napkin. "Cousin Allen over in Rockwall has been working on a new feed that he's been giving his chickens. He says they'll soon be laying eggs that are low in cholesterol. It's been tough giving up eggs, but I'm trying to follow doctor's orders. I plan on investing in the distribution of those eggs when Allen gets the go ahead to market them. We'll all make a pile of money.

Rod, I'll bet you've never been to a chicken farm. I'll take you out to Allen's place when we drive you back to Dallas next week."

"How was Sunday school this morning, boys?" asked Aunt Ruby.

"Oh you know, Miss Moon can't keep the class under control. She sent Johnny Jones to Reverend McCracken's office again after he hit Amanda Huggins with a spit wad. Alice Lee stuck her tongue out at Miss Moon. And Gayla Purdy totally made mincemeat out of the books of the New Testament when Miss Moon asked her to recite them from memory."

"I talked with Gayla's momma after church. She is at her wits' end with that gal. Gayla is painting her face with all that makeup and sneaking out at night to cavort with older boys. It can only lead to no good. Did you see how tight that skirt was that she was wearing in church? She was such a sweet child. A girl's reputation is her most precious possession. Her best friend, Alice Lee, imitates whatever Gayla does. Did you notice how revealing the clothes they wear are? It's so easy for a girl to get in trouble and bring disgrace to herself and her family. Do you follow what I'm saying, Rodger?'

I nodded yes, but I meant yes to a different question than the one she was asking.

"Alice Lee's brother, that Harvey Lee, is hanging around with a bunch of good-for-nothing troublemakers. There's talk that instead of holding down jobs and bringing in some money for their families, those shiftless boys in his crowd have been shoplifting and breaking into cars. They've been racing their cars late at night, too. Let's hope no one ends up in jail or gets killed. Sakes alive, the Lees are a good Christian family, but they don't know what to do about Alice and Harvey."

"Momma, next Sunday, can I stay home from church with Daddy?" pleaded Mark.

"I pray to the Lord that your Daddy will change his mind about going to church. How I worry so about all our souls. You, young man, will continue to attend Sunday school. Also, I want you to come with me to prayer group this Wednesday night."

"Aw, Momma."

"Ruby, honey, this Wednesday night the rodeo will be over in Bogata. I'm planning on taking the boys. I hope that will be all right with you. No trip to Texas is complete without seeing a rodeo."

"Yippee-yi-yo-ki-yay! Roddy, Red River County is the rodeo capital of the world. I can't wait to see those buckin' broncos. You should see the cowboys ropin' those steers. Momma, you promised I could go this year," pleaded Mark.

"My stars. I guess since cousin Roddy is visiting you can miss prayer group this once."

"Thanks, Momma," Mark said as he got up and playfully wrapped his arms around his mother. She laughed as she wriggled free from his grasp.

"Would you like some more fried chicken, Mr. Rowdy? There's plenty more of everything out in the kitchen. I baked a chocolate layer cake, and it looks delicious. Save some room for that," said Aunt Ruby's housekeeper Myrlie, as she hurried about picking up empty plates and making sure we were all fully satisfied with our meal.

"Miss Ruby, I'm so sorry, but I need to hurry home early tonight. My little girl Lula Mae gave birth to a baby boy last night. She's just a baby herself and is still hurting pretty bad. That girl doesn't want to nurse the young one. She was laying in bed crying this morning when I left, and Grandma Sadie is getting too old to mind the tiny ones."

"Why, Myrlie, I had no idea Lula Mae was pregnant. My, oh my. Why, she's only fifteen years old. Come to think of it, she hasn't been around here helping with the chores for quite a while. I should have known something was wrong. What can we do to help you and Lula Mae?"

"Lord have mercy, Miss Ruby. I'm so embarrassed. I tried to teach that gal to stay away from boys. But these children today, they don't listen. Seems like colored boys never take no for an answer.

"When her water broke last night, I called Grandmama Sadie to bring the new life into this troubled world. Of course, no white doctor in these parts would deliver a colored baby. Why, Grandmama delivered both Lula Mae and me. Nearly every colored child in these parts was brought into this world by my grandmama."

"Lula Mae howled and howled with each labor pain. She cried, 'Make it stop, Momma. My insides are splitting open. It hurts too much. Please, God, let me die.'"

"When I saw Lula Mae going out with that sweet-talkin' Dawson boy, I warned her not to let him go too far. I tried to teach that child about the birds and the bees. I told her what my Momma told me: 'It feel good going in, but it don't feel good comin' out.'"

"It took ten hours, but that darling baby boy finally came out. How that girl did scream. Now I have one more hungry mouth to feed and a baby to help raise at my age. Lordy, Lordy."

"My stars. Myrlie, please take all that chicken and those vegetables home with you. You know where the extra blankets are in the top of the closet. Take those home. Come over to the Hub tomorrow and Mister Harry will have some baby clothes ready for your new grandbaby. Now you head for home right now, and I'll clean up around here."

"Bless you, Mr. and Miss Wise. I'm so blessed to work for white people as fine as you. Tomorrow I'll do the pots and pans and get started on washing the windows."

"Never mind about that, Myrlie. You hurry home to your people right now," said Aunt Ruby.

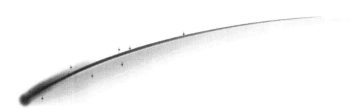

RODEO

"COME ON, BOYS. Pile in the car. It's rodeo time!" Uncle Harry shouted to us.

Mark and I raced out of the house and climbed into the Bonneville. Uncle Harry had the top down. The upholstery had a few spots on it from our driving-into-the-ditch adventure, but it was still the nicest car I had ever been in.

"The Bogata Rodeo is the biggest event of the year in these parts. Red River County is the rodeo capital of the world," Mark informed me.

"In Spanish class we learned to pronounce the capital of Colombia as BO-ga-ta. It's pretty funny that you Texans call it Ba-GOH-ta," I remarked.

"Yes sir, Texans speak our very own language. We call Detroit, Texas, DEE-troit. But Paris, Texas, is pronounced just like Paris, France. The food is better in Gay Paree, though. If you like towns with funny sounding names, just remember that down the road apiece, we've got a little crossroads called Bug Tussle, pronounced BUG-tussle," laughed Uncle Harry.

"Thanks, Daddy, for getting us out of Wednesday prayer meeting. It's even worse than Sunday school. I know I can be a good Christian without listening to Miss Moon carry on twice a week. Boy, I'd rather hear buzzards swirlin' over my head than listen to her drone on. Isn't going to church on Sunday enough?"

"We both owe your momma one for letting me take you out tonight. I know she's very worried about my Jewish soul. She never misses church and constantly prays for our salvation. If prayers are really answered, I have a feeling we're all heading for heaven someday."

"Daddy, you know that we are only saved through our faith in Jesus."

"Okay, Mark, enough about that right now," Uncle Harry interrupted. "Let's pray some local boys make us proud and take the top prizes tonight. Time to show my Florida nephew some genuine Texas fun. A rodeo is like a county fair, a circus, and a Wild West show all rolled into one. It's not far from here. We'll be there in three shakes of a lamb's tail."

We pulled into the unpaved parking lot at the Bogata Rodeo Grounds. It was full of rundown cars, motorcycles, and pickup trucks. Many of the trucks had gun racks in the back with shotguns and rifles on display. I couldn't help but notice all the Confederate flag decals on windows and bumpers. One bumper sticker had a Confederate flag with the slogan "Fergit? Hell No!" Another said "Support Your Local Ku Klux Klan." Still another read "Impeach Earl Warren. Repeal Brown vs. Board of Education." Coral Gables this was not.

The wonderful smells coming from the small midway made my stomach start to growl. We hadn't eaten anything since lunch. "Would you like to try a corny dog on a stick, Roddy?" asked Uncle Harry.

"Sure. They smell great, and I've never had one before."

"Let's have two and smother them with mustard," said Mark.

I totally enjoyed my hot dogs buried inside fried cornbread meal and was ready for the next treat. "That corn on the cob smells great. Can I try one?"

"Sure, Roddy. Let's each have one. Make sure you put plenty of butter and salt on it," said Uncle Harry, as he reached for his wallet yet again.

We each had an elephant ear, which is fried dough batter folded over to look like an ear. It was so greasy that even my stomach, usually fueled with Royal Castle and Burger King burgers, Frankie's pizza and Arbetter's hot dogs, was starting to do a combination of the Twist and the Mashed Potato.

"Let's grab a big bag of kettle corn before we head to the viewing stands," said Uncle Harry.

"Hey, look over yonder! There's J.B., showing off at the High Striker. The idea is to ring the bell by smashing a platform with a large mallet and show everyone how strong you are," said Mark.

"Step right up and show the girls that you're a he-man. Just ten cents, one thin dime, for your chance to ring the bell," cried the barker.

"Let me try, Daddy. I know I'm stronger than I was last year," begged Mark.

"Okay, boys. One try each. You go first, Roddy."

I picked up the mallet, raised it over my head, and slammed it down as hard as I could. My aim was a little off center, and the ball only went about halfway up the pole. It passed the levels of Sick Duck, Wimp, and Nice Girl and stopped at Nice Try Young Fella. It was humiliating not being able to ring the bell and show that I was a real man. I guess having a bar mitzvah didn't confer manhood in every way.

"Let me show you how it's done, Roddy," Mark said, as he slammed the mallet down with all his might right in the center of the platform. The ball went up the pole past where mine had gone and reached the level of Big Boy. "That's better than last year, but I know I'm stronger than that. Can I try again, Daddy?"

Uncle Harry reached into his pocket and laid down another shiny, silver, Roosevelt dime. Mark slammed the mallet down again, but the ball only went slightly higher than the time before. It was above Big Boy and almost to the line rating him a He-Man.

"Okay, Rodger the ol' codger, it's time to watch a real man show some muscle," said J.B., as he rubbed his hands together and pulled his shoulders back. J.B. raised the mallet high over his head and slammed it down right in the middle of the platform. The ball went up, up, and up, past Sick Duck, Small Fry, Good Girl, Nice Try, Big Boy and He-Man. It went all the way to King Kong, rang the bell, and lit up a red light.

"All right. We have a winner. A real Texas strong man. Give your girlfriend this Kewpie doll, pardner."

J.B. strutted around and flexed his muscles. "How do you like them apples?" he bragged. "Have fun at the rodeo, fellas. See you at the store, Boss."

"Nice hit there, J.B. Mark and Rod want to go waterskiing down at North Lake. Would you take them out on my boat next Saturday?" asked Uncle Harry.

J.B handed the young woman he was with the Kewpie doll. She was wearing shorts and a halter top that showed off her very curvaceous figure. I couldn't help but notice her slim, well-shaped legs that were accented by the spiky high-heeled shoes she was wearing. Silken brown hair extended halfway down her back. She turned in our direction and smiled at Uncle Harry. Then I noticed she was missing one of her upper front teeth. As J.B. sashayed off, arm in arm with his sexy but gap-toothed gal, he replied in his nasal Texas drawl, "Sure enough. Happy to oblige, Boss."

✿ ✿ ✿

"C'mon, Dad, let's find a seat. I don't want to miss the Grand Parade," urged Mark.

"Okay. Look, there's your Uncle Clyde. We can all sit together," said Uncle Harry as we walked up to a tall man wearing a cowboy hat, blue jeans, and leather cowboy boots. "Howdy, Clyde. Great to see you. I want you to meet my sister Jenny's boy, Roddy. He's here visiting us from Miami."

"Pleased to meet ya there, Rodney," drawled Clyde. "MI-ami? You're a long way from home. I'll bet your Uncle Harry's showing you a great time."

"He sure is. I'm excited about seeing my first rodeo. Do you sometimes pronounce it rode- AY-oh?" I asked.

"Rode-AY-oh? Rode-AY-oh? Anyone who can't say rodeo the proper Texas way gets taken over to Paige's tree," laughed Clyde as he hitched up his pants.

"Paige's tree? What's that?" I asked.

"He's kidding around, Rod," said Mark. "Clyde's always been a big joker. Paige's tree is the oldest tree in Clarksville. It's also called 'the hangin' tree'. It's the tree where they used to take criminals to execute them in the old days. I don't think anyone's been hung for at least 50 years, but there are dozens of stories from the old days, when lynching was instant justice, Texas-style."

"Rodeo is part of our Texas way of life," Clyde continued. "Only a Yankee or fancy Hollywood type would say rode-AY-oh. And they better not talk like that in these parts. Ain't that the truth, Harry?"

"Sorry, just asking," I said, while simultaneously trying to cover my mythical Jewish horns and protecting my tender neck from an imaginary noose.

"Harry, why don't you bring the boys out to the ranch tomorrow? We'll be tenderizing some bull calves. Moooo! We'll have a barbecue and maybe crack out the shotguns."

"Great, Clyde. I'll bring the boys out in Pa's old Studebaker."

I could hear the piccolo solo from "The Stars and Stripes Forever" being piped through loudspeakers into the rodeo arena as we walked in. We took our seats in the bleachers as the crowd clapped and stomped in rhythm to Sousa's rousing march. There was red, white and blue bunting everywhere. The smell of horses, bulls and steers that were penned up below us pervaded the entire arena. It was like sitting on a mountain of primitive animal energy swelling up and ready to be released.

"Ladies and gentleman, cowboys and cowgirls, it's showtime! Let's welcome the Red River Riders as they lead the Grand Parade. Let's get this rodeo started! I'm Larry 'Lariat' Tyler, your rodeo announcer."

The gates to the corral opened and out pranced twenty-four beautiful horses ridden by cowgirls in red cowboy hats and short, pleated red skirts. They weaved the horses in and out of intricate formations without ever bumping into each other. After several minutes of precision riding, they formed two straight lines, with each girl standing on her saddle. Out marched cowboys twirling lassoes and clowns with painted faces and floppy shoes. There were American, Texan, and Confederate flags everywhere.

"Please stand while the Bogata High School band plays 'The Star Spangled Banner' followed by 'The Eyes of Texas'."

Out marched a pitifully small band of about thirty high school kids in crooked lines. There were plenty of clammed and squawked notes, but they were overshadowed by the enthusiastic singing of the crowd. Everyone held his cowboy hat over his heart.

"Before our first event, we'd like to thank the generous sponsors who helped make this Bogata Rodeo possible: the Clarksville Fire Department, Tyler Pontiac, Crazy Horse Western Wear, Ponderosa Liquors, Dairy Queen, and last, but certainly not least, Clarksville's own Hub. Hometown service at hometown prices. Why travel to Dallas or Texarkana when you can shop right here at our own Hub?"

A few spectators clapped, and I heard a few whistles from the crowd. Clyde slapped Uncle Harry on the back as my uncle beamed with pride and said, "That's my store."

"Our first event is for the young'uns. I want all you children age ten and under out on the field for the Calf Scramble. A prize of five dollars for the child who captures the most yellow ribbons."

Ten calves with yellow ribbons tied to their tails were released, and about thirty children scrambled about, trying to pull the ribbons off. The crowd laughed as some kids boldly approached the young cows, and others shied away from the more reluctant calves that balked and kicked. After about five minutes, an older boy waved four yellow ribbons above his head.

"Step right over here and take this five-dollar bill, young fella. Let's have a hand for our prize-winning veal buster and future bronco buster," the announcer crowed as the audience laughed and applauded. "Our next event is Bareback Bronco Riding. Each contestant will try to stay on a wild bucking bronco for eight seconds. Points are also awarded for style. Charlie McDuff is up first. John Wayne Scott, you're on deck, and Buck Travis, you hang around."

The gate was opened and Charlie McDuff came out with one hand waving in the air. The horse reared and bucked, and Charlie went down hard on his head and neck in about two seconds as the crowd gasped. The bronco kicked hard, and its rear hoof just missed Charlie's face. I thought he must be paralyzed or at least seriously wounded, but he brushed himself off and headed back behind the fence. The rodeo clowns came out and lured the bronco back to the corral area.

Next came John Wayne Scott. He fared only slightly better, lasting about five seconds. He also appeared to hit his head against the dirt very hard. He got up slowly, shaking and rubbing his head, only slightly stunned. I thought I knew how he felt. I once got a concussion from falling out of a tree. I hit my head so hard that I literally saw stars. I missed three days of school waiting for the bruises and cuts to start healing. I knew TV wrestling was fake, but there was no way these tough rodeo guys could fake this.

"Buck Travis is a rodeo champion, Rod. Watch him ride. There's not a horse in all Texas he can't stay aboard," said Uncle Harry.

Buck's horse bucked wildly. Buck held on to the reins with one hand and waved the other in the air, trying to stay on the wild bronco. The horse spun round and round but was not able to throw the rider. The buzzer went off, signaling that eight seconds was up. Buck jumped off his mount and waved to the crowd, who applauded and cheered with appreciation. We all knew that no one would get a better ride on this night.

I watched as Buck walked back toward the stands. He blew a kiss to the crowd, and responding with a kiss of her own was none other than Gayla Purdy, sitting next to redheaded Alice Lee.

Next, we watched young cowgirls compete in Barrel Racing. Teenage girls wearing cute western outfits competed to see who could ride their quarter horse accurately, in a tight cloverleaf pattern around three barrels. Points were awarded for speed and deducted for knocking over barrels.

We watched as several contestants ran the course, each knocking over several barrels. The final contestant, the smiling and very pretty Franci Beth Marsh, galloped through the course without touching a barrel. She rode with style and grace. Her almost-perfect score was highest of the night. Uncle Harry, Mark, and Clyde all cheered when the smiling Franci Beth held up her first-place trophy.

"Franci Beth is a Clarksville gal," said Uncle Harry. "Her daddy put her on a horse before she could walk. She's been winning horseback riding competitions all over Texas, and she sure is making us proud. Rides like a dream. What a great future she has as a star on the rodeo circuit.. Good-looking, too, huh? Your cousin Mark has had his eye on her for a long time. She bought that outfit at the Hub just last week."

Franci Beth waved in our direction as she walked back to the stands. Mark stood up, pressed two fingers against his lower lip, and gave the loudest wolf whistle I had ever heard. He waved back to Franci Beth enthusiastically.

"Next up is y'all's favorite: steer wrestling. Our sponsor for steer wrestling tonight is Green Mint Snuff. A little pinch inside your lip gives you that great tobacco flavor. Please be polite and use a spittoon whenever possible."

We watched as a steer was released and a cowboy on horseback chased it. "That second cowboy is called a hazer. He helps guide the steer, so the first cowboy can grab it," Mark informed me.

The cowboy jumped down from his horse, grabbed the steer by the horns, and threw it down to the ground. Whoever could accomplish this the fastest was the winner.

"I could use a hazer and steer wrestler like that tomorrow when we fix the bull calves. I could also use the help on branding day," declared Clyde. "Tomorrow we'll be tying down those bull calves. Some of them weigh nearly 350 pounds."

Clyde watched the next event, tie-down roping, with great appreciation. "It's great to see a young cowhand who knows how to handle a lasso. I still know how to do plenty of rope tricks. In fact, there's not a calf on my ranch I can't catch. I can still throw them down, too.

"I'll bet you've never lassoed a calf, have you there, Rodney? We can check out your cowboy skills when y'all come out to the ranch tomorrow."

"Ladies and gentlemen, cowboys and cowgirls, our last event tonight will be bull riding. The most dangerous bull of all time, Bodacious, is snortin' and stompin' down in the pen. He is 1500 pounds of vicious animal. With us from Broken Bow, Oklahoma, just across the Red River, is Guy Strong. This brave cowboy will try to be the first person to ever ride Bodacious for eight seconds. Eight long seconds." An eternity, I thought.

All eyes turned to the pen where three cowhands held onto the twisting, snorting bull, while Guy mounted him. Guy nodded his head, and the gate was opened. Out roared Bodacious, circling, shaking, and bucking with all his might. Guy held on for two, three, four, five seconds, but then was thrown violently to the ground. Bodacious immediately turned toward Guy and began to gore him with his sharp horns. The cowboy curled up into a ball and tried to protect his head with his arms.

As the crowd gasped, two clowns leaped out of barrels and began waving red sheets and capes at the bull like toreadors. The bull turned toward the clowns as they jumped up and down and blew whistles. As soon as the bull turned toward the clowns, Guy got up, ran to the side of the corral, and jumped over the fence. His clothes were torn, and we could see that he was bleeding from his side.

The brave clowns ran toward the gate leading to the pen that Bodacious had come out of. They waved sheets at the bull, trying to lure him back into the pen. As the bull charged them, the clowns jumped out of the way, and one of them barely missed getting gored. Cowhands opened the gate at just the right time and managed to capture the furious bull.

"These cowboys and clowns deserve a big hand, folks. Guy's going to be all right. Let's give a big Texas holler for all these rodeo performers. That was the last event of the tonight's show. Ya'll have a great night and tell your friends about the thrills you've had tonight at the Bogata Rodeo. This is Larry 'Lariat' Tyler, wishing you all a good night."

"Wow, that was great, Uncle Harry. I had a fantastic time. Thanks for bringing me," I said as we climbed down from the bleachers.

"My pleasure, Roddy. Would you like another corny dog or elephant ear for the ride home? How about a funnel cake?"

"No, thanks." I burped, feeling my stomach now doing the Cha Cha. "Do you think Aunt Ruby might be able to find me some Alka Seltzer?"

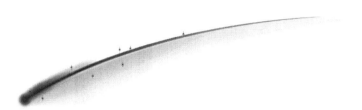

C H A P T E R   1 7
BARBECUE AND BUCKSHOT

THE NEXT DAY, we drove out a dusty Texas country road to Mark's Uncle Clyde's ranch.

"Clyde's got 500 head of cattle grazing out here. He's mighty proud of this four hundred acre spread. He's a real Texas country boy who has done very well for himself," said Uncle Harry.

"Clyde's great grandfather fought for the Confederacy in the Civil War. When the war ended, he came west from Mississippi to Texas because he didn't want to live under Yankee occupation. He bought a small patch of land and farmed it. They never were able to grow much more than they could eat and always remained very poor. Clyde inherited a few acres when his daddy died.

"The best thing that ever happened to him was falling in love with Ruby's sister, Violet. They got married right about the time I started making good money at the Hub. As a wedding gift, I bought Clyde a bull and four heifers. He bred his small herd, bought the surrounding land, and now runs this great cattle ranch. But no matter how big he gets, Clyde's really just an old-fashioned Texas cowboy with old fashioned ideas."

"I heard they were making steers today," said Mark over the sound of gravel clacking against the underside of the Studebaker as we pulled up to the ranch.

"What do you mean, 'making steers'?" I asked naively, as Uncle Harry slammed his door shut and slapped Clyde on the back.

"City boys don't know nothin' about castrating bulls," remarked Clyde, as he sized me up with a glance.

"Castrating?"

"Removing their balls, so the meat will be more tender," snickered Mark.

"Balls?"

"*You* know. Their testicles. Where the male hormones come from. No one wants to eat the meat of a bull. It's too tough. And once they're fixed, they'll leave the cows alone."

"Thanks for the biology lesson, Mark. This is all news to me," I replied, as I tried to digest this new information. I felt a slight ache in my own groin thinking about the plight of the poor young calves that would never mature to be bulls.

"Ya'll hungry? I've already got hot charcoal on the barbecue. Burgers and other delicious treats. What do y'all barbecue down in MI-ami, Rodney?" asked Clyde.

"Hamburgers, hot dogs, and sometimes Dad will grill some steaks."

"Think cousin Rod would enjoy some Rocky Mountain oysters, Mark?" asked Clyde.

Mark laughed out loud as I did a mental geography lesson, puzzling over where in Colorado one might find oysters.

"Set down at the picnic table while I throw these on the fire," said Clyde, as he reached into a bucket of raw meat, flattened out a grey patty, and added it to the already sizzling burgers.

"After we eat, we're going to do some target practice. What's your favorite weapon, Rod?" asked Mark.

"Dad had a couple of pistols up in the attic that he brought back from the war. They disappeared after Mom caught us playing with them. I've never really fired a weapon." I admitted.

"Well, then, I guess you'll need a lesson in gun safety before we start target practice," said Uncle Harry.

"Let's eat them while they're still bloody," laughed Clyde. as he handed me a thick meat sandwich on a bun.

"I put plenty of mustard and ketchup on there for you, Rodney. Time to chow down on a Texas speciality."

I hesitated before biting into the odd-looking burger. I was a guest on this ranch and didn't want to insult my host by refusing the food so generously offered. I noticed the others watching me as they bit into their hamburgers. As I bit into it, the burger kind of squished in my mouth. I immediately spat out a disgusting chunk of meat, revolted by the taste and texture.

"What? You don't like Rocky Mountain oysters?" Mark howled, as they all doubled over with laughter.

"Son, that's how we put hair on a city boy's chest. You just ate barbecued bull's balls. Why don't you try one of these delicious burgers made from beef raised right here on this ranch," said Clyde, as he finally stopped laughing.

Retching, I replied, "No thank you, sir. I seem to have lost my appetite."

✿ ✿ ✿

I was still feeling queasy, embarrassed, and mad as a raging bull, when Clyde suggested we walk over to the field they used for target shooting. Several rifles and shotguns were standing in a small shed. Clyde pulled out two. "This is a .22 rifle, and this is a 12-gauge shotgun. You know the difference between a rifle and a shotgun?" he asked.

"Not really," I replied flatly.

"A rifle shoots out a single shell," Mark explained. "The caliber of the rifle is a measurement of the diameter of the bore. So this .22 is twenty-two hundredths of an inch across the barrel. The higher the caliber, the larger the shell.

"Shotguns are measured by the amount of shot that comes out of the shell. The larger the shot, the lower the gauge. So this 12-gauge is a very powerful weapon. Let me show you how to work the safety."

Mark handed me the shotgun. He showed me how to work the little lever that was the safety. "Unless you're firing, always keep the safety engaged. Guns are perfectly safe if you just follow some simple rules. Never point a gun at anyone. Even if you know it's empty, always assume that it's loaded. Keep the weapon pointed toward the ground, but don't point it at your own feet."

"Seems simple enough," I said. "None of my friends have guns. But I guess out here in Texas everyone is a cowboy, just like in the movies."

"Guns keep us free," said Clyde, while poking me in the chest with his index finger. "Every red-blooded American needs to have a gun. We have to defend ourselves. Some day the Russians will come try to turn us into Communists. That's when every man jack will take to the hills with his guns and run the foreigners out of here."

"Yes," added Mark, "the left-wing bureaucrats and Communists in the government keep trying to make laws to force people to have licenses and take classes in shooting before they can buy a gun. I'd like to see them try to take away my rifles. I know how to defend myself and my family."

"I guess you're right. I never really thought of it that way before," I said, although I was less convinced than I tried to sound.

"When we get home, I'll show you some neat gun magazines I get from the National Rifle Association. Daddy let me join up now that I turned thirteen."

"Okay, Rodney, I got you all set up here," said Clyde as he handed me the shotgun. "You don't point a gun, you aim it. Put the butt of the barrel against your shoulder and look down the barrel. Those beads sticking up from the barrel are your sights. Line up the beads with your target. That Coke can on the fence is your target. Let's see if you have enough lead in your pencil to knock that can off the fence."

The shotgun felt very heavy as I lifted it to my shoulder. My heart started racing, and there was a pulse in my ears as I lined up the beads with the can.

"Hold the butt hard against you. That 12-gauge has quite a kick," Mark whispered to me.

I felt beads of sweat gathering on my upper lip and in my armpits. How dangerous could it be to shoot a can off a fence? Bracing myself hard, I squeezed my eyes shut as I squeezed the trigger.

Kabloom! Suddenly there was smoke everywhere. Instantly, Uncle Harry jumped over and grabbed the shotgun out of my hands. I looked at the fence and saw that the can hadn't moved a bit. I was surprised that I didn't feel the kickback against my shoulder.

"I can't believe I missed. Darn! Can I have another try?"

"Roddy, the shotgun shell blew up in the chamber. The gun malfunctioned. I've never seen that happen before," said an astonished Mark.

I looked down at my shoes and noticed hundreds of little metal pellets on the ground. They were buckshot from the exploding cartridge. Many of the hard fragments were caught in my socks, and I could feel them against the soles of my feet. I brushed pieces of shot out of my hair. The air still smelled of smoke.

"Young man, don't you ever pick up a gun again! You and firearms make a bad mix. I hope you never have to fight in a war. You'd be a danger to your unit," said Clyde.

"I really hope I don't have to fight in a war, but I hope I'd be brave. Dad always said that he froze his butt off fighting the Nazis under General Patton in Belgium, France, and Germany, so that his sons would not have to go to war," I said, feeling a little bit mystified since I was not the one who had maintained or loaded the shotgun.

"That's right, Roddy," said a shaken Uncle Harry. "I hope my boy never experiences the horror of war. I can't begin to describe the Battle of Okinawa. So many Japs committed suicide rather than surrender to us. Conditions were terrible as we fought from island to island knocking the enemy off the territory they had conquered. I still miss the buddies I lost taking those Pacific Islands. We also lost men to malaria. I was so sick with fever that I couldn't lift my head off my cot for days. Lucky for me, my malaria hasn't acted up in a few years."

"Gosh, Uncle Harry, no one ever told me that you fought in the Pacific. I knew Dad saw some horrible things with the Third Army as they mopped up the Nazis and met up with the Russians at the Inn River in Austria at the end of the war. I once overheard him talking with a war buddy from his unit in the 71st Infantry

Division. They whispered and cried about the time they liberated a concentration camp. Since he spoke Yiddish, German, and French, Dad was one of the first U.S. soldiers allowed into the camp. He said the skeletal Jewish victims were so insane with hunger that they were eating dirt and tree bark."

"Yes, Roddy, my generation witnessed horrible cruelty inflicted by the Germans and the Japanese. I don't know which was worse, the war against Germany or the war against Japan," said Uncle Harry, pursing his lips together in a grimace and shaking his head sadly.

"You would never know that my brother, your Uncle Will, is a hero. He's only alive today because he was smart enough to disobey an order.

"He was aboard the USS Franklin the day it was attacked by a Japanese dive-bomber. Two bombs had struck the aircraft carrier right at its most vulnerable spot and caused enormous damage. Fully-fueled planes blew up on the deck. There were fires everywhere. Ammo and bombs exploded and created infernos across the carrier. It was sheer hell.

"The order was given to abandon ship. Your Uncle Will watched many men jump overboard and lie motionless in the water after a ten-story fall. Then he spotted the circling dorsal fins. Many times he has told me what he had been thinking while contemplating obeying the order to jump. He said, 'I may die today, but it's not going to be from slamming my body into the Pacific Ocean. I am not going to be shark food, either.'

"Willie was among the brave sailors who stayed aboard and manned the fire hoses. He also helped rescue some of the crewmembers who were trapped below deck.

"The Franklin was listing badly, and they thought she was going to sink. Miraculously, however, the fires were contained just enough to keep her afloat.

"The Franklin was adrift in the water and floating toward the mainland of Japan. Somehow, she was saved and towed to safety and eventually was able to steam back to Pearl Harbor.

"Over 700 men perished that day. Most of the men who jumped or were blown overboard into the Pacific died. There were terrible stories about shark attacks. Of the men who stayed aboard the carrier, most suffered burns, but over 700 survived.

"I was visiting Willie in the hospital on Okinawa, the day President Truman dropped the A-bomb on Hiroshima. We were overjoyed that the war was over. We knew that many innocent people died in that mushroom cloud, but we justified it as revenge for the surprise attack on Pearl Harbor and the terrible treatment of our POWs. Everyone was relieved that we would not have to fight the Japanese on their home islands. That would have been the bloodiest battle of the war. There would have been countless casualties on both sides.

"Even though it took months for Will to recover from his painful burns, I never once heard him complain about his injuries or express hatred for the Japanese."

Uncle Harry put his arm around me and said, "Let's hope there's never a World War III and that you boys can grow up in peace." My uncle tousled my hair, and a few more shotgun pellets fell to the ground. Then he brushed a few remaining pellets from my shoulders. There were even a few pieces of shot in my eyebrows. Lucky for me, I had my eyes tightly closed when I squeezed the trigger.

As we hopped back in the Studebaker for the ride back to Clarksville, I noticed Uncle Harry's hands were trembling, and his eyes were glistening with tears. His skin had turned a ghostly shade of gray, and his shirt was soaked with sweat.

"I almost killed my sister's boy," he muttered to himself, as he shifted the reliable old Studebaker into third gear and accelerated down the road home.

CHURCH PICNIC

AUNT RUBY AND Uncle Harry walked hand in hand toward the town square in the center of Clarksville. It was obvious they enjoyed their life together. Mark and I lagged behind, comparing schools in our hometowns.

"You're so lucky to be starting high school in the fall," I said, thinking about another year in the junior high band and wishing I could march with the Southwest Miami High Royal Lancer Band.

"I don't know," replied Mark. "There are fights nearly every day after school at Clarksville High. The older guys like to pick on the smallest ninth graders. No one messes with me, though, because I'm a big guy and have already shown that I know how to deal with bullies and other future convicts. I try to serve as bodyguard for the little guys and make sure none of my friends get pushed around.

"At least I'll get to be in the high school band. I think we get to take a couple of road trips to games this year, and I know who I want to sit on the bus with. I can't wait to hold her in my arms, and hug and kiss her. Franci Beth is a great horseback rider, and she's captain of the twirlers. I know she likes me, too. She's in eleventh grade and told me about what goes on in the band bus after the lights go out. I know I'll be able to get my sweetheart to sit on my lap. Yeah, yeah."

"Franci Beth, a rodeo star and the head majorette. Wow. She's so cute. You lucky devil, you," I said, as I gave Mark a light punch in the shoulder.

"It'll be fun marching at Bulldog football games, too. Coach begged me to go out for the football team. Old Coach Jumpin' Jimmy Joplin has been the Bulldogs' coach since the Stone Age. He talks real slow like a good old Texas boy. That's why everybody calls him Deputy Dog.

"After all these years of coaching football, though, he's still no judge of talent. I'm a darn good quarterback, but Jumpin' Jiminy would probably put me on the offensive line knockin' heads with the biggest guys in Northeast Texas. I'm a lover, not a fighter.

"Football? I'll stick with touch. Who needs to walk around all bruised up? Non-contact activities like band, Future Business Leaders of America, and the Four-H Club are more to my liking.

"What we need at Clarksville high is a water skiing team. Grade nine? Algebra and chemistry are killers. And Latin? It's Greek to me. I'm sure not ready to start thinking about college."

There were a couple of old, banged-up, yellow church buses waiting in the town square. These were the dinosaurs we were going to ride in out to the church campgrounds for the picnic. We climbed aboard our bus. It smelled like the boy's locker room at Riviera Junior High in Miami. The seat covers were worn down to the springs, and there was no air-conditioning, of course. The windows were open as wide as possible because it was such a hot day. This clunker made my Greyhound out of the Coral Gables bus terminal seem like a ride on presidential Air Force One.

I recognized several of the kids from Sunday school. Mark grunted hello to a few guys. Gayla and Alice Lee were seated in the back. They were both wearing Bermuda shorts and tops that left their bellies exposed. They did not look up from their conversation as Mark and I boarded. It seemed like we were invisible to them.

We sat down a row behind J.B., who was chatting and laughing with several of his friends. "I rang the bell and lit up the light on the High Striker. Won my gal a Kewpie doll. Ain't that right, Rodger Dodger?"

"Looking strong there, J.B.," I replied.

"I also know how to handle a shotgun. Heard you had another adventure out at Clyde's. City boy's getting an education, sure enough. Can't drive a car and can't fire a shotgun. You couldn't hit a target even if you had a magic bullet. Looks like trouble always knows where to find a city slicker like you."

Looking out the window, I noticed three young black men walking on the other side of the town square. J.B. leaned out the open bus window and yelled, "Hey, you boys! Why don't you go back to your own side of town? Move it quick or me and my friends will drag you over to Paige's tree and have ourselves a hangin' party. Get out of my sight right now. I'm warnin' ya."

One of J.B.'s friends at the front of the bus yelled out a familiar and ugly racial taunt. Another shook his fist and then ran his index finger across his neck twice as a threat to slit the black boys' throats.

"Hush right now! Junior Boy Bowden, you shut that foul mouth of yours," Aunt Ruby scolded, as she gave J.B. a hard slap on the shoulder. "That's no way to talk. We're going to a church-sponsored event. All people are the children of God, no matter what their color."

Uncle Harry stood up and grabbed J.B.'s two friends by the front of their shirts and pulled them out of their seats.

"Listen up, Harvey Lee and Oswald Wallace. We don't want trouble here in Clarksville. We're a peaceful town.

"Word travels fast around here. Johnson Creech told me y'all are up to no good and are hanging out with a bunch of Klansmen and ex-cons over in Bug Tussle. Well, Fannin County Sheriff Gerald Fitz is an old friend of mine, and I'm of a mind to call him up and tell him to keep an eye on you two troublemakers."

"Them colored boys was making eyes at our white girls sitting on this bus. I'll string 'em up myself if they don't stay away from our people," piped up Harvey Lee.

The young Negro men glanced around nervously, lowered their heads, and rapidly moved around the corner and out of our sight.

"The times are a changin' boys. This isn't your daddy's world," said Uncle Harry, still gripping Harvey Lee and Oswald by their shirts. "I don't want to hear that kind of talk. Those young black men were just walking by. You know they didn't harm anyone.

"I don't like hearing threats like that coming from this church bus. We have to live and let live. That kind of talk is a disgrace, and it embarrasses me in front of my nephew."

"Okay, Harry. You're the boss," said J.B. derisively. "I guess that's why you got elected mayor of this town. You always have to be fair to everyone.

"But just so those boys know, they better stay on their own side of town. You got colored kids in your school, Nephew Rodg?"

"No, my school in Miami is all white. We have dozens of Cuban kids, though, because so many people had to escape from Fidel Castro and Communism. My Cuban friends told me how Castro took their homes, their parents' businesses, and all their money.

"There were rumors that Castro was going to round up all the young boys and send them to work camps in the Soviet Union. Operation Pedro Pan was set up by the United States government and the Catholic Church to rescue the boys from Cuba. It helped 14,000 Cuban kids escape to freedom in Miami.

"There are thousands of Cuban children who came to Miami without their families. They haven't seen their parents for years. Can you imagine leaving your home and family for a country where you don't even speak the language? Some idiots at school make fun of their Spanish accents.

"I don't have a problem at all with the schools being integrated. I'm even trying to learn Spanish."

J.B. looked at me, shook his head, rolled his eyes, and sneered in his thickest Texas drawl, "You talk like a Yankee. You talk through your nose."

✵ ✵ ✵

The buses rolled down country roads for about an hour. Finally, we came to the spot where the church picnic was being held. The ground was rolling with gentle hills. The campgrounds were surrounded by woods and shaded by large trees.

Young children were running around playing tag. A little blonde girl with freckles and pigtails ran after a chubby little boy and finally tagged him. Then she pushed him down on the ground and kissed him on the cheek. He wiped away the kiss with his shirtsleeve like it had cooties. The little girl ran away laughing, and the little boy got right up and chased after her.

I could smell the charcoal and hickory fires grilling hamburgers, hot dogs, chicken, and ribs. Aunt Ruby sat down at a picnic table beside her sister. Clyde was tending to the burgers.

"I know you like 'em rare, Rodney," he laughed. "How many burgers are you hungry fer?"

"Uh, no thank you, Clyde. I think I'm going for the potato salad and coleslaw. Maybe munch on a few chips and save room for those good-looking cherry pies I see over there."

"You sure, now? It's the finest beef. Raised right here in Northeast Texas."

With the memory of Rocky Mountain oysters still fresh in my memory, I wondered if barbecue was ever going to appeal to me again.

Mark and I gulped down our dinners. Then we then joined the guys tossing the football around.

The ball was whipped to Mark. He caught it, yelled "Go long, Rod," and did a little pump fake. I sprinted as fast as I could down the field, and Mark threw a perfect pass. He put it right over my shoulder, and I caught it in stride, making a fingertip catch look easy.

I looked over and there were Gayla and Alice Lee sitting on a fence with a couple of guys. Gayla looked at me and clapped her fingers together very daintily, congratulating me on my long catch. Then she turned and put her arms around Buck Travis, rodeo star. Next to her, Alice Lee was locked in a long kiss with

Guy Strong. He looked fully recovered from his bout with the horns of Bodacious, the killer bull.

Buck held Gayla close to him. I watched as he put his hands on her round fanny and pulled her in close. She straddled his leg with hers and ground her hips into him. He bent down to nibble at her neck. They looked like were madly in love with each other. "Oh, man," I jealously muttered to myself. Then I trotted back to the huddle and threw a 20-yard spiral on a rope, complete to my cousin Mark.

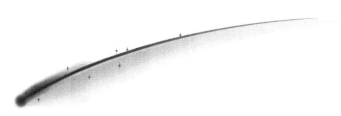

CHAPTER 19

BURNING A CROSS

THE SKY WAS streaked crimson red and burnt orange as the sun slowly dropped below the horizon. I focused my eyes on the glowing disk that is the source of all life. Copernicus proved centuries ago that the sun is stationary, and it is the earth that rotates.

For a brief but cosmic moment, I perceived his truth that the sun is fixed in the heavens. The sight of the sun setting in the west was actually the earth rotating away from the sun. For the first time in my life, I experienced the movement of our planet. It felt like a revelation.

The air grew cool and crisp, and I wished I'd brought a long-sleeved shirt. We joined the crowd gathered at the head of a trail that led up the hill and into the woods. Reverend McCracken began singing and church members joined him in song, as we slowly walked up the trail and away from the clearing where the picnic had been held.

"There's a church in the valley by the wildwood
No lovelier place in the dale
No spot is so dear to my childhood
As the little brown church in the vale."

The rest of the church group formed a line as J.B., Clyde, and several other men lit torches and led the entire gathering of picnickers up the hill. The light of the torches cast shadows on the trees, which looked like the walls of a natural cathedral. As the torches flickered in the wind, the shadows of the singers danced like spirits. It felt like we really were in a church in the wildwood.

We walked deep into the woods and up the hill. We stopped, still singing, and came to a small clearing. Several people sang sweet harmony. I didn't know the words to the hymn, but I tried to sing along with Aunt Ruby and Mark.

"Oh, come to the church by the wildwood
Come to the church in the dale
No place is so dear to my childhood
As the little brown church in the vale."

The crowd gathered around a large wooden cross that had been erected on a small, grassy knoll. It was at least ten feet tall.

J.B. stepped forward with his torch and set the cross on fire. It had been doused with kerosene, and it burst into bright golden flames. He threw his arms up and pumped his fists wildly like he was celebrating a victory. These Christians were burning a cross. Burning a cross! Was this a Ku Klux Klan rally? It seemed more like an ancient pagan ritual. The fire snapped, crackled and popped as sparkling embers rose into the night sky. Everyone had a beatific smile on their faces as they began to sing again.

"Amazing grace, how sweet the sound
That saved a wretch like me.
I once was lost and now I'm found
Was blind and now I see."

The stars began to come out on this cool, clear night. I listened carefully to the words of the most beautiful hymn I'd ever heard. Some people raised their hands joyously in the air.

I stood next to Aunt Ruby as she, Uncle Harry, and Mark held hands and sang. Voices rang out sweet, joyous, and strong. Clyde and Violet, and even Gayla and Alice Lee and their rodeo star boyfriends, Guy Strong and Buck Travis, swayed together and sincerely sang praise to God as the sky grew darker.

"When we've been here ten thousand years
Bright shining in the sun
We've no less days to sing God's praise
Than when we've first begun."

The cross continued to burn brightly. This was not a Ku Klux Klan rally. This was an expression of religious devotion and of the unity of the members of the Clarksville Christian Church. I was an outsider, but I felt welcomed in this group.

The flickering fire of the burning cross illuminated the faces of the assembled crowd. A sparkling light caught my eye. It was a reflection of the fiery burning cross glistening from Aunt Ruby's simple gold cross necklace. Another flicker caught my eye. The six-pointed Star of David that Uncle Harry wore as his belt buckle seemed to glow with a supernatural golden light.

I looked into the clear, moonless sky, gazing at the constellations and the Milky Way. I had never seen them so clearly. Aunt Ruby touched my hand to get my attention. She pointed to the sky as if she were introducing me to God's greatest creation, the infinite heavens. Suddenly, at the exact point where Aunt Ruby's finger was pointing, a shooting star burned across the sky, leaving a tracer of light still visible long after its brilliance disappeared beyond the horizon.

Startled by its intensity, we reacted like a crowd at a fireworks display: "Ooooh, aaahhhhh." My mouth dropped open in amazement. Lifting her hands and turning her palms up toward God, Aunt Ruby cried out "Hallelujah!"

"Hallelujah!" echoed the crowd.

"Hallelujah!"

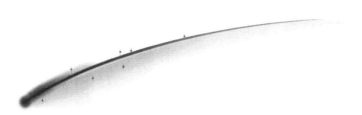

NORTH LAKE

"WHY WOULD A Florida kid come to Texas to learn to water ski? It don't make no sense." J.B. spoke in his grating nasal voice. I guess he was trying to talk like a Yankee. It seemed like he was mocking me, and it was starting to get under my skin.

"This is a really cool boat. Look at that outboard motor. I'll bet it really moves fast. I want to drive it. Mark, you're so lucky to have your own boat."

"You'll get your chance Rod. Help me load these skis. I'll drive first and you can ski," said Mark as he climbed aboard.

"Watch out for water moccasins. A Cajun boy got bit by one a couple years ago and nearly died. They're poisonous and have sharp teeth, Rodgie," cautioned J.B., with a sly grin on his face.

"Water moccasins? Maybe I'll just ride in the boat."

"Don't worry, Rod. We ski here all the time. Have fun and don't think about snakes," Mark reassured me, as he started the motor, backed the boat out expertly and then took us around the lake a couple of times.

North Lake was actually a reservoir located about four miles out of town. The isolated, clear blue lake was almost completely surrounded by thick green forest.

Mark pointed to a pile of rocks near the shore and warned, "The water's real shallow over by those rocks. A girl fell off her water skis in a couple of inches of water last year and got paralyzed. Stay away from that part of the lake. Just make sure you don't ski near the rocks."

Once we were out in deep water, Mark cut the engine, and the boat glided to a stop. I jumped into the lake. The water was cool and refreshing.

I fumbled clumsily with the skis. It took a while to finally get the rubber foot molds on my feet and get my toes pointed up parallel with the skis. Mark threw me the line and started moving the boat forward. As he sped up, I started to stand but almost immediately lost my balance, toppled forward, and lost my skis. Mark drove around. He picked up the skis and threw them back to me.

"Lean back hard and let the boat do the work. It's easy. Keep your tips up and out of the water," he shouted.

Mark gunned the boat, and I felt it pulling me out of the water. I tried to relax and lean back.

"All right. I'm up. I'm skiing." I held on as the boat pulled me halfway around the lake. The wind blew through my hair. What a sense of accomplishment, freedom, and exhilaration all at the same time. Skimming over the smooth surface of the water behind the boat I wondered, "Is this is what surfing feels like?"

Mark gave me a thumbs up and sped up the boat. "Lean to the right and jump the wake," he yelled.

I pulled to the right and went right through the wake. Now I was skiing outside the wake where the water was much rougher. The skis slapped hard against the choppy surface of the lake. My knees were like shock absorbers, but my teeth still chattered together.

Mark waved to me and yelled, "Jump that wake."

Leaning back to the left, I attempted to cross back over the wake. My ski tips dug into the water, and down I went, face first, choking on a mouthful of water. I coughed, sputtered, and spat out the lake water. Mark brought the boat around, reached his hand down, and pulled me into the boat from the top rung of the ladder.

"Had enough for now? It's my turn. I want to ski, too. Watch and learn."

Mark picked me up and drove back to the dock, where J.B. was standing with his hands on his hips. J.B. jumped into the boat and took charge of the wheel.

Mark put on the slalom. Both feet fit on one ski, one in front of the other. He sat down at the end of the dock, with the slalom hanging over the edge.

J.B. threw Mark the line and accelerated the boat in a hurry. When the line tightened, Mark stood up, slapped his ski into the water, and started skiing right off the dock.

Mark jumped the wake several times. We were really moving fast. Holding the rope with one hand, he turned around and skied backward for a while. Then he whipped back around, skiing like an old pro.

J.B. brought the boat back around toward the dock. He glanced over at me, grinning, as he pushed the accelerator forward as far as it would go and headed straight for the center of the dock. Mark was being steered to disaster.

Suddenly, kicking up a spray, the boat veered hard toward open water. Mark dropped the line as he sped straight ahead. Lifting his ski tips, he slowed himself down and coasted like he was Jesus walking on water. With perfect timing, he turned to one side and sat down gently on the edge of the dock. What an impressive show of talent and bravado.

"Okay, Rodger Dodger. Your turn to show off. Let's go. I'll drive the boat," said J.B.

Mark climbed back in the boat, and J.B. took us out to the middle of lake. I jumped in the water, put on my skis, and grabbed the tow rope. This time I let the boat pull me up. We started heading toward the swampy side of the lake. Unlike Mark, who let me learn to ski at a moderate speed, J.B. accelerated the boat to top speed. I quickly lost my balance and did another face plant near some cattails.

The boat moved away from me as I swam around hunting for my skis. I looked over toward the swampy shore and saw something move. Water moccasin! It must be an enormous snake from the way the water was rippling away from it. It was moving in my direction. Where was that boat?

J.B. was joyriding around the lake, happy to let me float and wait. He was in no hurry. I felt something swimming near me. It bumped me in the side. Way too large to be a snake. It was a huge alligator!

My heart started racing as panic set in. I was certain I was going to be pulled under water and eaten alive. I had just became a man, and now I was going to die in this godforsaken swamp. I should have stayed home this summer. I had to be a big shot and travel to Texas.

As the boat approached, the alligator kept swimming across the lake. I could see its powerful tail undulating like a wave, propelling the alligator rapidly away from me.

"Alligator!" I yelled to Mark and J.B. "Alligator!"

They were both doubled over with laughter. "That's just Old Pete. He swims by here every day about this time. He never bothers nobody, no how," howled J.B.

"There's a twelve-foot alligator in this lake!"

"C'mon, Rodge Podge, you scaredy cat. Grab that rope," J.B. taunted. Then he took off again, pulling me faster and faster. I didn't feel real steady and had to fight to stay on my skis.

J.B. started pulling me toward the rocks that Mark had warned me about. I tried to steer away from the shallow area but did not yet have full control over my skis. Suddenly, the rocks just under the surface were brushing the bottom of my skis. The water was only a few inches deep. It felt like I was skiing over a gravel road.

I started to lose my balance. Oh, no. That poor paralyzed girl must have lost control of her skis at the same spot. I flailed my arms round and round trying to stay on my skis. Somehow I fought hard and barely managed to hold on and avoid a terrible fall.

In a few more seconds, I was back skiing in deep water. Mark was looking back at me as I let go of the rope and let myself gently down into the water. My heart was still pounding when the boat came back around and Mark helped me get back in.

Shaking his head, Mark said, "Sorry, Roddy. You really had a close call with those rocks. I was really afraid you would get bloodied up, or worse." Turning to J.B., Mark frowned and said abruptly, "Move over, Junior Boy. This is my boat, and I'm driving it now." With fists clenched, the seething Mark bumped J.B. hard with his shoulder, shoving him away from the wheel.

His pink skin turning red, J.B. shrugged and looked down at his feet, perhaps feeling a sense of shame. Not looking at either of us, he weakly muttered, "Okay, boss."

✡ ✡ ✡

After our adventures in waterskiing, we decided to go for a swim. Mark dove off the dock like an arrow and barely made a splash. He yelled, "C'mon, Rod, let's swim out to the raft."

It was about thirty strokes out to a wooden raft. We climbed the ladder and dried off in the warm Texas sun.

"It's a good thing you didn't fall off the skis in the shallow water. You could have been paralyzed or even killed. I can't believe J.B. pulled you over there."

"J.B. doesn't seem to be that fond of me. Maybe because I don't talk like a Texan. I guess I better start saying 'y'all', and 'yes ma'am' and 'no ma'am', like y'all do."

"J.B. isn't always warm and friendly to folks who aren't from around here. Some of his lowlife buddies have been bragging about plans to make sure the schools around here don't get integrated. He helps out a lot at the Hub, but Daddy won't be too happy to hear that you, his favorite nephew, had another near disaster that was pretty much J.B.'s fault. On the other hand, he'll get a laugh out of Old Pete scaring the bejeezus out of you."

"Don't get J.B. in trouble on my account. Your dad told me that he's a great employee. Do you think he really meant to hurt me?"

"As the Bible says, 'Let he who is without sin cast the first stone.' After seeing that shooting star last night, I am going to be the best Christian I can be from now on. God showed you a sign last night, Rod. You need to accept Christ as your savior if you want to go to heaven. Let the Lord into your heart, and you'll never have to fear anything."

"It was a meteorite, Mark, though I must admit that it was the most amazing sight I've ever seen, and I said 'hallelujah' along with everyone else. But I still find it hard to believe that faith in Jesus is the only path to heaven."

"That's what it says in the Bible, and I know everything in the Bible is true."

"That means that all our Jewish relatives are in hell or are going there? Grandma, Grandpa and Uncle Shuki? Do you think they're all burning in hell? They were the sweetest, kindest people. I can't believe God would punish them for being the wrong religion. What about your kind, generous dad? Don't you think he'll be in heaven waiting for you when you kick the bucket?"

"The Bible says that salvation is only possible by being a Christian. Open your heart, Jesus will enter it, and you will be born again."

"How about the poor innocent children who died in Nazi Germany? Do you think they're in hell? Did the Jewish soldiers who died fighting for our country's freedom get sent to eternal fire? If Hitler and his henchmen let Jesus into their hearts, did they get to go to heaven? It makes no sense to me, no sense at all."

"No Nazi could be a true Christian in his heart and then murder innocent people. Rod, think of it like an insurance policy. What have you got to lose? If you believe, you get eternal life. Why take a chance on going to hell? Believing in Christ is an insurance policy that pays off when you die, with eternal life in heaven."

"I just finished eight years of Sunday school and five years of Hebrew school. The most important teaching in Judaism is that God is one. The first commandment tells us to have no other gods before us. God is not an idol or a man. He is the universal spirit. Do you expect me to go against my own religion, my rabbi, and the religion of my parents and grandparents?"

"Just have faith. I'm going to pray that God grants you and Daddy grace. If you have grace and an open heart, Jesus will enter your heart, and you will believe in him as your savior and be saved."

The sound of splashing distracted us from our deep religious discussion. Gayla and Alice Lee were standing on the dock. Both of them were wearing teeny bikinis. Galya's was white with yellow polka dots. Alice Lee's bikini was yellow with white polka dots. Guy Strong and Buck Travis were nowhere in sight. The half-naked girls dove into the water and started swimming out to the raft.

Mark started quietly singing Brian Hyland's song about the girls who were afraid to come out of the water because they didn't want anyone to see their itsy, bitsy, teeny weenie bikinis. He sang completely out of tune, but his eyes were wide open, staring at the exposed skin and womanly curves of the two girls he had grown up with. He walked out to the end of the diving board and did his best swan dive right toward the girls. Following his lead, I stood on the board, puffed out my chest, sucked in my stomach, and performed a perfect jack knife.

The girls watched us dive and then swam up to the raft. They went under water and swam into the space under the raft.

"Hey, you. The water's nice and warm, and it's kind of dark under here. Come on and join us," Gayla said enticingly.

"I can't believe it," Mark whispered to me.

We dove into the water like darts. We quickly swam down and came up under the raft. The water was up to my chest, so we could all easily stand.

"Did you have fun at the picnic? We sure did," said Alice Lee.

"That shooting star was a sign from heaven. It was awesome," said Mark.

"How about you? Are you having fun?" asked Gayla, as she came up close and wrapped her legs around me.

Remembering where Buck Travis had his hands at the picnic, I immediately grabbed her fanny with both of mine. Gayla cooed a little bit and snuggled in close to me. I let my fingers inch under her bikini bottoms. Her skin was amazingly soft and smooth. Alice Lee, ignoring Mark, came over to me and wrapped her legs around me too. I was the meat in a girl sandwich.

"Hey, Robbie from Florida. It's just like the song says: '*Two girls for every boy*'," Alice Lee whispered in my ear. Her warm breath in my ear sent a shiver through my body.

"Alice Lee, his name isn't Robbie. It's Rod," Gayla said, as she pressed her knee gently between my legs. "I think from now on we'd better call him Hot Rod."

Snuggling and cuddling under the raft with two girls. My only thought was, "There is a God, and right now I'm in heaven."

✤ ✤ ✤

By the time I finally dried off, it was late in the afternoon. J.B. had disappeared, and so had our chances for a ride. Mark suggested that we walk back to town so that we wouldn't be late for dinner.

"Gayla and Alice Lee with you under the raft," Mark said, shaking his head. "I figured the best thing I could do was swim back to the dock and leave you at their mercy, you devil, you."

"Mercy, mercy, mercy. Time passes so fast. It's unbelievable that tomorrow is my last day in Clarksville. It's been so much fun. Alice Lee and Gayla attacked me under the raft. Gayla and I kissed until my jaw started aching. Alice Lee is plenty experienced, and she sure isn't shy.

"They really want to come to Florida. They made me promise to take them surfing off of South Beach. I'd love to have more time with them. If I could stay a while longer in Clarksville, I could have Gayla as my girlfriend. But what if we ran into Buck and Guy? That would be more than awkward, and maybe even a little dangerous. Those two sure are lucky guys."

"Rodeo cowboys have schoolgirls to make out with in every town the rodeo goes to. Cuz, you made out with Gayla and Alice Lee at the same time. Just like Jan and Dean promised. Two to one. Two girls, one guy!

"Next summer, I'm coming to Miami, and you're going to teach me to surf. It's a sure way to get girls to like you. Two girls, one guy. Surfing. Is it as easy as waterskiing?"

"Mark, old boy, it's time for a confession. I misled you just a little bit. Do you think lying is an unforgivable sin?

"Truth be told, I don't technically, surf. I don't have my driver's license yet, so I don't get to the beach too often. I mean, I've jumped up and down in some huge whitecaps, and I've had some really good rides bodysurfing. Sometimes my friends and I throw down pieces of plywood, jump onto them, and try to skim along in the shallow water near the shore. That's almost surfing, you know.

"I've watched plenty of the older guys surf near the pier at South Beach. Maybe someday Dad will let me buy a surfboard. I just know I'm going to be a great surfer."

"You don't really surf? No Surf City USA? What a scam! Gayla will be interested in hearing about that. No, wait. I can't say that I blame you for fakin' it. Telling girls that you surf seems like a sure way to get them to like you, so I guess it's okay. Yeah, your secret's safe with me. I won't tell Gayla the truth about my surfin' cousin. I can't wait to get into the ocean. Surfing looks just like a big old slalom. Next summer we'll be kings and rule the waves on Miami Beach."

CHAPTER 21
BITSY AND BAGELMAN

W E DIDN'T GET back to Mark's house until late in the afternoon. Mark checked the mailbox and pulled out a pile of letters and magazines. He quickly thumbed through them and handed me an envelope hand-addressed to me. Surprise! It was from Stevie Bagelman. I sat down on my bed and immediately ripped it open, eager to hear how things were back home.

Hi-Ho Rodgerino,

Your mom gave me your cousin's address. I'm writing to let you know what's happening back here in the sun-and-fun capital of the world since you got on the Greyhound and disappeared from your hometown.

I guess no one should be surprised that your good buddy and bodyguard, Wood the Hood, is in jail. We all knew he was a member of FCA, Future Convicts of America. Your friend and neighbor is only fourteen, and he's already locked up in the hoosegow. You've gotta admire a guy who doesn't let common sense deter him from his destiny.

Anyway, here's the story: Clifford Glick, in a moment of pure insanity, got into a poker game with Wood and some of his hoodlum friends. Glick started winning tons of money and made the mistake of mouthing off about it. He won several huge pots without even having a winning hand. Then he called Wood a sucker for falling for his bluffs. Of course, that made Wood go off like an intercontinental ballistic missile. He hauled off and started punching Cliff in the face. Glick was spitting out blood and broken teeth. His jaw was broken in two places, and he ended up with three teeth knocked out. He spent a couple nights in the hospital, and now his mouth is wired shut. Clifford's face is bruised and swollen and looks a lot like silly putty.

You know how Glick's mom is. She called the cops and decided to press charges on the Woodman. The cops came, surrounded the house, and finally had to drag him out in handcuffs. Then they took him off to Kendall. Wood hates cops, and once he got to Kendall, he punched a cop and blackened his eye. It took five guards to drag him into a cell.

My dad says Wood must have a little problem with authority figures. Since he was so out of control, they finally decided to lock him up in the county jail with the adult criminals. I'm afraid he's going to be in there for a long time. Doesn't look like his step-dad has any intention of bailing him out.

Here's something else you'll being interested in hearing about. Last Saturday, Bitsy and I decided to meet in the Gables and go to the movies at the Miracle. I wanted to see "Lord of the Flies", but Bitsy wanted to see Frankie and Annette in "Beach Party". We compromised and ended up in the back row of the balcony, watching "Bye Bye Birdie". Well, *sort* of watching the movie and sort of...well...*you* know.

Anyway, you've got to see it. Great songs, and Ann-Margret was super sexy just like she was in "State Fair".

You'll never guess who sat down in the balcony two rows in front of us: Helen Christofilaki was with Carl Hiaasen, that goody-two-shoes we had English composition with last year. I think they both go to Christian Youth Ministry or something like that. But here's the good news for you: Bitsy and I watched him work up the courage to put his arm around her. First, he scratched the back of his head and then he stretched out in a fake yawn. Working ever so slowly, he casually stretched his arm around Helen. The instant his hand came down on her shoulder, she grabbed it like it was a live anaconda and pulled it off of her.

Carl thought he was heading for paradise, but I think Helen is hell-bent on getting to heaven by being a good girl. They shared popcorn but nothing else. It looked to me like she was cold as a cherry Popsicle for the rest of the movie

When you get back home, I'll tell you everything about sitting in the balcony with Littlebit. I wouldn't dare put it down in writing. As a matter of fact, you have to destroy this letter as soon as you finish reading it so that it doesn't fall into the wrong hands.

Let me just say that your cousin sure is crazy about Tootsie Rolls. In fact, she's coming over to my house tomorrow night to listen to records with me. I've got all the cool makeout songs lined up and ready to go. Chances are awfully good that we'll listen to Johnny Mathis sing "Chances Are".

Anyway, I better go soon. I'm sure you're behaving yourself, young man. How are those Texas honeys? Are you being true to Helen? How's the music in Texas? Do they listen to rock and roll, or is it just country-western out there? I'll bet you're wearing spurs and riding horses, and rounding up the cattle with your Texas cousin. Seen any cowboys or Indians? Roy Rogers? Dale Evans? The Lone Ranger and Tonto?

Maybe when you get home you can ask Helen to come over and listen to us play guitar. I must say I admire your taste in girls. She sure is pretty. But don't worry. You can trust ol' Steverino. Believe me, I have my hands full with Littlebit.

So write back, or better yet, come on home. We're going into ninth grade. It'll be so cool when we rule that school.

As John Glenn said from earth orbit, "Roger, over and out."

Your pal,

Steverino

CHAPTER 22
BUG TUSSLE

I WAS TIRED AND hungry. As I daydreamed about Mom's cooking and hanging out with my friends back in Miami, a pang of homesickness washed over me. I took a long, refreshing shower and then stretched out on my bed and relaxed. I slept about forty winks.

The smell of trout frying in the kitchen wafted through the house, and I woke up famished. Clyde had been fishing out at North Lake and had a great day, even by his standards. He dropped off ten whopping trout and said that it only amounted to half of the catch. Myrlie cleaned them, filleted them, dipped them in breadcrumbs and eggs, and then fried them in a pan.

I looked over her shoulder and watched them sizzle. There was a mouthwatering aroma throughout the house. Fish had never tasted better. It was the best I ever ate.

After finishing dessert, we walked out to the front porch with our bellies stuffed and satisfied. Uncle Harry pulled out a couple of guitars and handed one of them to me. It was a blonde Gibson—the kind you drooled over in the music store window. Smiling contentedly, Uncle Harry sat down next to Aunt Ruby on the front porch swing. She reached over and tucked a pillow behind his back. It was these little acts of kindness that led me to believe they were deeply in love.

"Do you know how to tune a guitar, Rod?" asked my musical uncle, as he plucked the low E string on his Martin twelve-string and tightened it slightly. "Here's a pick."

I hit the low E on my guitar and tuned it to Uncle Harry's. EEEEE, AAAAA, DDDDD, GGGGG, BBBBB, EEEEE. We tuned up together until our guitars sounded just right. Uncle Harry began to strum a progression of chords in three-quarter time. They sounded so rich on that twelve-string. He started singing:

"Oh give me a home where the buffalo roam
and the deer and the antelope play."
I strummed along, and we all sang together.
"Where seldom is heard a discouraging word
and the skies are not cloudy all day."

Uncle Harry switched from singing melody to singing harmony, and Aunt Ruby joined me on the melody:

"Home home on the range
Where the deer and the antelope play.
Where seldom is heard a discouraging word
And the skies are not cloudy all day."

Uncle Harry continued strumming while I picked out the melody on the Gibson. The next time through the tune, I tried to embellish the melody a little bit.

"I wish I could play guitar like that. How long have you been picking guitar, Rod?" asked Mark.

"Pretty much as long as I can remember. I have a banged-up old six-string at home. My buddy Steve and I usually play blues and rock and roll tunes. We enjoy playing folk music, too. I've listened to the Kingston Trio's album *Live at the hungry i* so much that I have the whole album memorized. I'm sure you've heard Peter, Paul and Mary pick guitars and sing amazing harmony. Even my little sister has the words to "Puff the Magic Dragon" memorized. This Gibson is so easy to play and has such a full sound."

"Daddy and Momma sing like nightingales, but I can't carry a tune. I love to listen, though. Play us one of your favorite tunes, Roddy."

I started to strum the Gibson and sang the words to Woody Guthrie's tune:

"This land is your land, this land is my land.
From California to the New York Island"

Everyone joined in singing, as Uncle Harry deftly finger-picked the Martin.

"From the Redwood Forest to the Gulf Stream waters
This land was made for you and me.
As I went walking that ribbon of highway
I saw above me that endless skyway
I saw below me that golden valley
This land was made for you and me."

We played and sang together, and I picked out a lead. Uncle Harry skillfully used three fingers Travis picking. His intricate picking was obviously the result of years of guitar playing.

As we finished the tune, a maroon Cadillac Eldorado with huge tailfins and rocket-ship taillights slowly drove down the street and turned into the driveway of the Wise family.

"My stars! I wasn't expecting anyone to drop by tonight. Isn't that Reverend McCracken's car?" asked Aunt Ruby, straightening her skirt and combing her hair out of her eyes with her fingers.

"I sure hope he isn't going to beg me to come back to church," said Uncle Harry. "Lord help me, I might say something that I'll regret later."

"Now, Harry, you know the good Reverend is just trying to do God's work. We must extend him our hospitality."

Reverend McCracken climbed the porch steps of Harry and Ruby's white house slowly and deliberately. He had a grim, downcast expression on his face.

"Good evening, folks. That's some mighty fine music y'all are making. So sorry to interrupt your peaceful evening. Harry, may I have a word with you?"

"Now, Reverend, I'm a grown man and have many things to do on Sunday mornings. I don't need to be lectured about church attendance."

"No, no, that's not why I came over, Harry. I need to speak with you about a very troubling development. This is something important you all need to know about," said Reverend McCracken, looking very serious. "Sheriff Gerald Fitz over in Bug Tussle just called me. He's been keeping an eye on Harvey Lee and Oswald Wallace ever since you spoke to him about them after the church picnic. He told me that Johnson Creech warned you that they were up to no good."

Reverend McCracken continued while looking directly into Uncle Harry's blue eyes. "Those two Clarksville boys, along with your employee, Junior Boy Bowden, have joined a vigilante group that meets secretly over in Bug Tussle. Fitz had a couple of police in plainclothes stake out the doublewide trailer they hang out in. When they spotted Harvey Lee moving weapons from his car to the doublewide, they got a warrant and then knocked the door down. Inside that dump, guns, ammo, and several sticks of dynamite were found. They've even stockpiled battery acid. Hitler's *Mein Kampf* and other racist books were there, too. When they arrested J.B., he started ranting about how he opposed civil rights for Negros. He was going on and on about socialists and communists. He says they will fight to the death against the integration of our local schools.

"I think they've already attacked the pets of people they don't like with acid. A Labrador Retriever owned by a Jewish man living in Sulphur Springs died of its burns. Can you imagine those lowlifes attacking animals?"

"Reverend, do you mean to tell me that it was J.B. who threw acid on my gentle old dog, Sputnik? Why, Junior Boy Bowden has been working for me for years. I've always trusted him. I was thinking that someday I might allow him to buy a piece of the

Hub like Mister Clark did for me. I can't believe he would do something so cowardly as to attack a harmless animal. I've been good to J.B. I swan, I swan, I Suwanee River, I don't know what I'm going to do. I don't know where evil like that comes from. Maybe you can explain it, Reverend."

"Harry, I'm sure you feel betrayed like Jesus when he was betrayed by Judas," said the reverend with a sad grimace. "You know J.B.'s daddy, Jimbo Bowden, was active in the Ku Klux Klan for many years. J.B. heard hateful talk against Negroes and Jewish people from the time he was a little boy. Mostly they just talked tough, threatened violence against colored people, burned crosses, and marched around in those ridiculous white sheets.

"Now J. B. and his miscreant buddies are in big trouble. The Fannin County police have found evidence that these Bug Tussle boys were conspiring to blow up the Zion African Baptist Church. Oswald Wallace was bragging about how many Negroes he was going to kill with his firebomb. They were out to destroy innocent lives and the peace of our community. Now they're sitting in the Fannin County jail hoping the magistrate will set a low bail. There was a ton of evidence in that trailer. I'm afraid the national press is going to find out about the church-bombing plot. Next thing you know, here come a slew of Yankee reporters asking all kinds of questions. Clarksville will get the wrong kind of publicity."

Uncle Harry interrupted, "This is terrible news. We don't need bombings around here. I thought the days of lynching and racial violence were behind us. President Kennedy is committed to greater equality for the races. The times are changing, and we must accept that in the coming years the old ways of segregation are going to pass away. Doesn't the Bible say 'Love thy neighbor as thyself'?"

"You're right. That's from the Book of Leviticus. The Old Testament, Harry. Those black Christian churches worship the same God we do. All of us are children of the Lord. An attack on a house of worship is an attack on God and an attack on all of us. I believe everyone deserves protection under the law, even if they're not white or Christian."

"Battery acid and dynamite. If I find out which one those boys hurt my pup, I'll brand him and turn him into a steer myself."

"'Vengeance is mine, sayeth the Lord.' Harry, you are a gentle man, and you will overcome your anger. As it says in Romans 12:21/20, 'Do not be overcome with evil, but overcome evil with good.'" Reverend McCracken began to raise his voice and wave his arms like he was preaching from his pulpit.

"Sure, sure, Reverend. You've got a proverb for everything." Uncle Harry held up his hands and turned the palms toward the reverend, trying to interrupt the impending sermon. Shaking his head sadly, he continued, "This is terrible news. I never imagined J.B. held a grudge against me because of my religion. We treated him just like a member of our family."

"I know this is hard, but we'll all be looking to you for leadership, Mayor Wise."

Aunt Ruby, Uncle Harry, and Mark all looked shocked and sad. They knew this was going to change their lives. Our peaceful evening had become dismal, and everyone on the porch was downcast. Each of us was in our own cloud of sadness and confusion,

Wanting to change the grim mood, I reached over, picked up the Martin, and held it in my arms. It was my first time playing a twelve-string guitar, and I attempted to imitate Uncle Harry's Travis-picking. The progression of chords in a minor key created rich harmonics on the twelve-string. I continued picking the Martin and started singing a song I learned in nursery school at Beth El Synagogue in the city of my birth, Akron, Ohio:

"Heenay ma tov oo ma nayim
Shevet achim gam yachad"

After hesitating for a few seconds, Uncle Harry started singing along. The words to the Hebrew folk song came back to him even after being separated from his Jewish roots for many years. Our voices blended together in harmony.

"Heenay ma tov oo ma nayim
Shevet achim gam yachad"

"Ah you're singing in the language of the Good Book. Can you translate those guttural Hebrew words into English for us, young man?" asked Reverend McCracken.

"Yes. It means 'How good and pleasant it is when men sit together as brothers.'"

"Oh, yes. Psalm 133. I'm very familiar with it. Young man, you're a fine musician. I'm sure the students in Miss Moon's Sunday school class would enjoy learning to sing a Psalm in God's language. We'd be delighted for you to bring your guitar to church next Sunday and teach your Christian friends a song of the Israelites."

"Uh, no thanks, Reverend. It's time for me to start thinking about my trip home. Tomorrow Uncle Harry is gonna drive me back to Dallas," I said, relieved that I would not have go to Miss Moon's Sunday school class again.

The Reverend stepped down from the porch and headed back to his car. Turning back to us, he said, "You come back and see us, young fellow. Ruby, Mark, and Harry, sorry to be the bearer of such bad tidings. Remember, the Lord moves in mysterious ways, and his goodness will overcome all evil. See you in church."

Aunt Ruby spoke up, "My stars. Church-bombing and burning our Sputnik with battery acid. What is this world coming to? I'm afraid these really are the end of days that are prophesied in the Book of Revelation. This world looks like it's headed for damnation. I worry so about all those A-bombs the Russians have pointed at us. I pray for the president to keep us safe. The Kennedys are such a lovely family. The president is a good Christian, and I hear he goes to his Catholic mass as often as he can."

"Listen to this, Aunt Ruby. I bet you recognize this song," I said, trying to change the subject from the grim news that the Reverend had brought us. Strumming the Martin, I sang out:

"If you miss the train I'm on, you will know that I am gone
You can hear the whistle blow a hundred miles,

A hundred miles, a hundred miles, a hundred miles,
A hundred miles
You can hear the whistle blow a hundred miles."

Her face brightening up, Aunt Ruby sang out like she was in church,

"Lord I'm one, Lord I'm two, Lord I'm three, Lord I'm four,
Lord I'm five hundred miles from my home."

Uncle Harry picked out the melody on the Gibson, as I continued strumming the chords. As he played, he revealed all the emotion in his heart, and when be bent a string it twanged "waaa ooo waaa" like the Texas drawls of the people of Clarksville, Texas. We all sang together, and the song took on a deeper meaning to me as I thought back on my long trip one thousand five hundred miles from my home:

"Not a shirt on my back, not a penny to my name
Lord I can't go a-home this-a-way
this away, this away, this-a-way, this-a-way,
Lord, I can't go a-home this-a-way.
If you miss the train I'm on you will know that I am gone
You can hear the whistle blow a hundred miles."

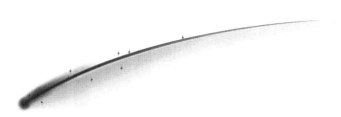

BACK TO DALLAS

THE NEXT MORNING, Myrlie knocked on the door of the bedroom I was sharing with Mark.

"Breakfast is ready, Mister Marky Mark. I made bacon and eggs, Mister Rowdy."

"Thanks, Myrlie," said Mark.

"The bacon smells great, Myrlie," I said as we sat down at the kitchen table. There were fried eggs, crisp bacon, slices of ham, grits, collard greens, and Texas toast soaked in butter. Even the toast is big in Texas. It was much thicker than regular sliced toast. Sweet and crispy, each piece of Texas toast was a meal itself.

"Here's your coffee. Just the way you like it, with cream and sugar. Don't forget to drink your juice and save room for peaches and cream."

Uncle Harry spoke up. "Are you all packed, Roddy? I sure wish you could stay longer. You've been a wonderful guest. It would be very helpful if you could stay with us until the end of the summer. Now that J.B. is sitting in a jail cell, we're shorthanded at the Hub, and we could use an extra worker. Ruby and Violet are mighty fine sales ladies, and they've volunteered to help out and work more hours until I can hire someone to take J.B.'s place. Mark, I know you don't like heavy lifting, but I'm going to need you back in the stockroom and on the loading dock. It's time for you to learn the retail business. You're going to be working at the Hub full time for the rest of the summer. When I retire, you'll need to be ready to take over as the owner of our store."

"Yes, Daddy," Mark responded, suddenly sounding like a much younger boy.

Myrlie returned to the dining room and began to clear the dishes.

"Myrlie," said Uncle Harry, "I'll be needing another worker down at the Hub now that J.B. has gotten himself in trouble with the law. I'd like to hire your boy Medgar to help us out. Mark will be needing an extra hand unloading the trucks and stacking merchandise in the stockroom. There are several other chores that will need to be done that J.B. used to take care of. I'm willing to pay close to the minimum wage if he would like to work part time for me after school."

"Oh, thank you so much, Mr. Harry. It would help our family so much to have Medgar working for you at the Hub. I'll make sure he's there tomorrow after school. He's a good boy. He'll work hard. Bless you, Mr. Harry, and bless you, Miss Ruby."

Aunt Ruby joined the conversation. "I feel so sad, and I am so terribly disappointed in J.B. Uncle Harry and I cried ourselves to sleep last night. We've been betrayed by a person we trusted. How could he have attacked our dog? Now he and those troublemakers he's been hanging around with are in a fix. They've been caught with dynamite and accused of planning to blow up a Negro church. First they attack an innocent dog. Then they plan to attack innocent churchgoing people. We live in troubled times. I'm so worried. I don't know what I'd do without the Lord's comfort."

"We'll be leaving soon. Ruby, Sweetheart, we're going to stop in Rockwall at Allen's chicken farm. I have a lot invested in those low-cholesterol eggs. So many folks with high cholesterol would love to be able to eat eggs without guilt. I'll drop Rod at Willie's and then head home. I probably won't be home until after dark. Try not to worry too much."

"Mama, next summer I'm going to Miami. I've got to learn how to surf," Mark informed his mother.

"My friends will love you. We'll tell everyone you're a real cowboy and a bull dogger. Mark, the Brahma bull rider. Make sure to bring a ten-gallon hat with you. If the subject of football comes up, we can say you're the quarterback of the Clarksville High Bulldogs."

"My son, the cowboy. Do you remember when we put you on a calf when you were about five years old? You were very brave and rode that heifer for about three seconds before she threw you. It was a hard fall, and you didn't even cry," laughed Uncle Harry.

"I'll never ride a killer bull like Bodacious, but I've loved watching the rodeo ever since," replied Mark.

Mark carried my bag out to the Bonneville for me. As we walked to the car, Sputnik ran up to us with his tail wagging behind him. He jumped up and tried to lick my face. I patted his side. The bald spot from the acid burn hadn't changed. It looked like the fur would never grow back. He was nothing but a hound dog. "So long, Sputnik the space dog."

"Down, Sputnik," commanded Aunt Ruby.

"C'mon, Spooter. Here, boy. Good old Spooter." Sputnik bounded to Uncle Harry, who petted his head and ruffled his fur. He gently pushed Sputnik down and allowed the grateful dog to lick his hand.

Mark threw my bag in the trunk and slapped me on the back. "See you next summer, Hot Rod. Drop me a line sometime and tell me about the surfer girls, you devil you. Two to one. Girls to guys. I like those odds," he said with a knowing wink.

"God bless you, and God bless us all. Give my love to your momma and daddy," said Aunt Ruby, as she hugged me warmly and then wiped a tear from her eye. "Never forget that God loves you. He showed you with a shooting star."

Uncle Harry drove us out of town. I had one last look at the Hub. We drove by Clarksville High and down the road past farms and ranches. We drove on toward Dallas, listening to country music on the radio. Uncle Harry sang along with the radio in his deep baritone voice.

"I just love that song about Abilene. It's true what it says about the women there. My Texas woman never treats me mean. There's nothing like country music, don't you think, Rod?"

"I'm more of a rock 'n roll fan myself. I guess country's pretty good, too."

"Goodness gracious. Rock and roll? That's all you young folks listen to. Listen to the tune they're playing on the radio now, 'Ring of Fire'. Johnny Cash really knows something about love and how it can change a person. That must be some wicked love affair he's singing about."

"Oh, yeah. I know this one. They play it all the time on WQAM in Miami." We sang together about the burning ring of fire. "Wow. What a great song. I understand what he's singing about. Johnny's burning in hell because of love. I like country music, too."

We drove on through several Texas towns, some so small they didn't even have a stoplight. Texas 66 was a country road. Large herds of cattle and horses grazed behind miles of well-tended fences. The countryside was quiet and peaceful.

"A chicken farm is quite different from a cattle ranch, but the basic idea is the same. Instead of milk and beef, we're raising eggs and chickens. Allen's a genius. He's discovered a feed for chickens that makes them lay low-cholesterol eggs. It's just a matter of time before we can market them. There are so many folks with heart disease and high cholesterol, and there's no effective medicine to help them. My doctor says if I want my blood pressure to come down, I have to live a less stressful life and go on a diet. It's been so hard to stop smoking. Your Aunt Ruby always knows when I sneak one. Allen and I are going to sell healthy, low cholesterol eggs to folks with high cholesterol and high blood pressure. I think we'll make a fortune."

After several hours of driving, we arrived at Allen's chicken farm. Uncle Harry parked the car next to a building that looked like a long warehouse. A couple of big German Shepherds strained at their leashes and barked at us, drooling and revealing their sharp teeth. As soon as I slammed the car door shut, the odor of the chickens washed over me. The smell was so intense that it even burned my eyes. Revolted, I pinched my nose and covered my mouth.

"Hey, Harry. Good to see you again, Roddy. Welcome to Rockwall. Our claim to fame is that we're the smallest county in the largest state."

Allen walked us through the chicken coops. There were hundreds of cages stacked from the floor to almost the ceiling. In each cage were two chickens. White bird droppings were everywhere. I was unprepared for the stench, the filth, and the terrible conditions that the chickens had to live in. The smell of ammonia was overwhelming, and it burned my eyes. Getting queasy from the revolting conditions, I gagged and then ran outside to get a breath of fresh air.

Stepping outside to join me, Allen explained, "There are five hundred chickens here that we are experimenting on. Each group of one hundred gets a different feed. There are some chemists and biologists at Baylor that are analyzing the nutrients in the eggs. The results so far are promising. Some of the eggs have less than half the amount of cholesterol found when traditional feeds are used."

"That's sounds great, Allen. So many folks have high cholesterol and aren't supposed to eat eggs. How long til we're marketing the healthy eggs to the public?"

"The problem is the FDA wants us to run tests for several more years. We're trying to deal with all the paperwork and red tape. We may have to feed the eggs to several generations of lab animals before humans will be allowed to eat them. Too darn many bureaucrats in Washington. There's not a dime's worth of difference between the Republicans and the Democrats. It may be a very long time before we are able to recoup our investment."

"Look on the bright side, Allen. If we can't market the low-cholesterol eggs, we can always sell the chickens for fryers. Rod, isn't Myrlie's fried chicken the best you've ever eaten?"

Still gagging on the stench, the thought of Rocky Mountain oysters flashed into my mind. Chickens in filthy cages. I swallowed hard to keep my breakfast from coming back up.

"Uncle Harry, I'm thinking about giving up meat completely. Starting right this minute."

Uncle Harry responded with a chuckle, "I've turned my sister's boy into a vegetarian. Roddy, it's getting late. Let's get you back to Dallas, cowboy."

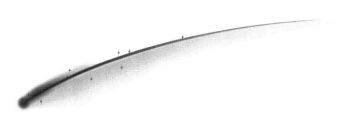

CAROUSEL

MARILYN GREETED ME with a hug around the neck and a peck on the cheek as I walked through the front door of her suburban Dallas house. "Did you have fun in Clarksville? Look at you, grinning like a Cheshire cat. Did you get yourself a small-town girlfriend? What were you and Mark up to, Rodya Raskalnikoff, you rascal?"

"Oh, you know, Marilyn. Church, Sunday school, and singing hymns. We had a blast at the rodeo. Mark taught me how to water ski, too. Did you know there was an alligator in North Lake?"

"Did Old Pete give you a scare?" asked Marilyn with mock sympathy. "I nearly peed in my pants the first time I saw him. He swims across the lake the same time every day. Those Clarksville kids act like he's their pet."

"I thought for sure I was going to be alligator food. Did you know that if you turn a gator on its belly and rub it, it goes to sleep? That gator was a lot bigger than me. I never could have won a wrestling match with him. Thank God he swam away from me."

Just then Suzy burst into the room holding the morning newspaper. "Look at this. There's an article about J.B. in the *Dallas Morning News*. He and those creepy friends of his are in so much trouble. They've been hurting people's pets, throwing rocks through the windows of Negroes, and harassing colored people all over northeast Texas. I never knew J.B. was so full of hate. He was always pleasant enough to Marilyn and me. He was a little rough with you, Rod, but he sure pulled us out of that ditch in a hurry."

"At the church picnic, he lit the burning cross and seemed to exult in happiness when it ignited. For an instant it felt like I was a Jewish boy at a Ku Klux Klan rally. Aunt Ruby and Uncle Harry would never support the Klan. Those church folks were singing songs of love and faith. They're just good Christians who want to share God's love with everyone."

I continued, "Uncle Harry, Aunt Ruby and Mark are so upset. They can't believe how wrong they were about someone who worked for them for so many years. Mark and I didn't even tell them how J.B. pulled me into shallow water when I was learning to water ski. I almost crashed on the rocks below the surface of the water. Maybe it was just his way of giving me a waterskiing lesson. Now it looks like he'll go to trial, and a judge and jury will decide if he goes to jail."

Marilyn interrupted me. "Listen, Rod, we have a very busy day today. We have to go to a travel agent downtown and buy your ticket home. I'm glad to hear that you're flying and not taking the Greyhound again."

"Yeah," I said, "Airline tickets are probably expensive, but it's going to be so exciting taking off on my first flight."

"Before we go to the travel agent, we're going to the Texas State Fair. It's always a blast. Suzy is bringing Donny Taylor. She thinks she is so cool talking about her "boyfriend". It's so cute. They have matching braces."

"If they make out, the dentist might have to cut them apart," I laughed.

"Remember Debbie Burns, who you sat next to on the way to drill team practice? She's not allowed to go out with non-Jewish guys. She's had to turn down dates from some of the cutest guys at TJ. She's starting to hate her parents, with all their stupid rules. It was her idea to make you the mascot of the drill team. I think she may have a little crush on you. Two blue-eyed Jews. A match made in heaven. She wants to come to the State Fair with us."

"Debbie's coming with us to the Fair? Marilyn, you're the best. Come to Miami over winter break. You can drive us all over town. We'll go to the beach, and you can become a surfer girl. You'll come back here with a tan that all your friends will be jealous of. You'll be fighting off the guys."

Sitting shotgun as Marilyn backed the Galaxy out of the driveway, I had to tease, "Don't drive us into a ditch, Parnelli Jones."

"Don't eat bull oysters, Jughead."

We picked up Donny and Debbie, who sat in the back seat with Suzy.

Debbie flashed a dimpled smile and informed me, "My grandma lives in an apartment off of Collins Avenue. I get to go to Miami Beach every Christmas vacation. Do you live near Collins Avenue?"

"Not that close, but when you visit, I'll take the bus from my house in South Miami and we can go to the beach. Surf City USA," I answered.

"You know they're really singing about California, Rodger. The really big waves are out west and in Hawaii. I'd love for you to teach me to surf, if the waves down there are ever big enough," Debbie said, flashing her big blue eyes.

"Or we can lay out on beach blankets and work on our tans. Then walk out on the pier and watch the fishermen. Sometimes there are some great shells that wash up on the beach. I've even found some shark's teeth," I replied as I turned completely around so I could smile at Debbie.

"It's so cool that they made a movie about the Texas State Fair. I've seen *State Fair* three times," she said.

"Twice," piped in Suzy.

"I liked it too," I said, as I started to sing:

"Our state fair is a great state fair
Don't miss it, don't even be late!"

Everyone in the car joined in:

"It's dollars to doughnuts that our state fair
Is the best state fair in our state!"

Donny busted out at the top of his lungs,

"I'm as corny as Kansas in August,
High as a flag on the Fourth of July!"

"No, no, Donny, that's from *South Pacific*," Suzy corrected.
Now Donny warbled like a crooner, his Adam's apple bobbing up and down.

"When you walk through a storm
Keep your chin up high
And don't be afraid of the dark."

"Donny, that's a song from *Carousel*," Suzy whined.
"Just testing to see if you're alert," Donny laughed.
"Roddy, do you remember this great song?" asked Debbie, as she chimed in with a strong voice,

"It's a grand night for singing,
The stars are bright above,"

We all joined in with her:

"The earth is aglow, and, to add to the show,
I think I am falling in love,
Falling, falling in love!"

"You be Pat Boone, and I'll be Ann-Margret," said Debbie.
"Suzy, you and Donny are Pamela Tiffin and Bobby Darin."
Marilyn gave an exasperated sigh, rolled her eyes, and sighed, "Oh, children. Puppy love is so darling."
Marilyn parked the car in the crowded parking lot. We got out of the Galaxy and weaved our way through the maze of parked cars into the fairgrounds. Debbie reached over and held my hand. We started to swing our arms back and forth like schoolchildren.

"Look! There's Big Tex. Just like in the movie," I pointed out the large mechanical cowboy that spoke in a very deep voice: "Howdy, folks. I'm Big Tex. Welcome to the Texas State Fair. Twenty-four days of food and fun."

"He's huge. I love his enormous cowboy hat," I said.

"Most cowboys wear ten-gallon hats. Big Tex wears a 75-gallon hat," Suzy laughed.

"Rodya," said Marilyn, "We need to get you a cowboy hat as a souvenir of Texas. Let's go over to that stand selling Texas clothing."

Marilyn picked out a ten-gallon hat and placed it on my head. "I'm buying you this. You are now an official Dallas cowboy. I dub thee, Sir Tex Noodleman."

We walked out of the hat stand and straight over to a building advertising pig races.

"Oh, look! They're having a greased-pig chase. Let's watch. I saw it last year and laughed so hard I got a stitch in my side," said Suzy, her eyes twinkling with excitement.

We sat down in the bleachers and watched as young children tried to catch piglets covered in grease. The antics of both the kids and the pigs were hysterically funny. Several kids fell flat on their faces in the mud as the pigs they were chasing slipped away. The audience laughed and applauded.

The smell of the pigs brought back memories of the chicken farm. My stomach began to churn. I thought, "Fruit, vegetables, and grains are delicious and nourishing food. Who needs meat, anyway?"

"I'm meeting a friend at the Comet. Who wants a ride the scariest rollercoaster in the world?" asked Marilyn.

"I want to ride the Comet. I just love scary rides. We'll have fun, fun, fun. Who are you meeting, Marilyn?" asked Suzy.

"Kenny Harris called me last night and asked me to meet him here at the State Fair. He wants to ride the Comet with me."

"Oh, a senior! And he's so cute. Let's go," said Suzy, as she led the way.

There was a long line waiting to get on the Comet. I watched the people riding it throwing their hands in the air as they went over the first hill. Everyone screamed as the roller coaster sped down the hill and around the bend. Nearly everyone was breathless and laughing as the ride ended. Some kids immediately got back in line to repeat the thrilling sensation. I was feeling a little nervous about the ride but tried to act nonchalant as we came to the front of the line. Kenny found us just as we were being seated in the rollercoaster. Marilyn pecked him lightly on the mouth. She grazed his lips with hers.

"Here we go. Donny and Suzy, you ride in the front car. Kenny and I will be behind you. Roddy and Debbie in the back," she commanded.

The ride attendant belted us in and cautioned us not to slip down in our seats. Debbie grabbed my arm with both her hands as we slowly went up the first hill. "I never ride scary rides. I'm terrified. Protect me, brave prince."

We held on for dear life as we roared down the first hill. The coaster raced down the tracks, and we were thrown in all directions. Debbie buried her face in my shoulder and screamed. With one arm around her, I tried to reassure and protect her. With my other hand, I held on to the safety bar for dear life. When the ride ended, Debbie massaged my bicep with both of her hands. "If you hadn't been next to me, I think I might have fainted. No more scary rides, please. Let's go ride the merry-go-round. It's more my speed."

Since a second round on the Comet was out of the question, we walked over to the famous and ornate Dentzel Carousel. It revolved slowly while calliope music played. Little children sat on the beautifully painted horses. A few couples sat in the chariots. "I'd rather not ride the horses. Let's sit in the dragon chariot," said Debbie, as we climbed on board.

I held hands with Debbie and put my other arm around her. She leaned against me and seductively petted my hand. She ran her fingers up and down my forearm then stroked each of my fingers with her index finger. She intertwined her fingers with mine and pressed her palm against my palm. She put her lips close to my ear and sang in a whisper,

"It's a grand night for singing,
The stars are bright above,
The earth is aglow, and, to add to the show,
I think I am falling in love,
Falling, falling in love!"

Debbie kissed me innocently on the cheek. Her lips were so soft. I closed my eyes and felt a shiver run up my spine. Just holding hands and receiving an innocent, gentle kiss from Debbie felt very romantic. My thoughts briefly returned to the attack of Gayla and Alice Lee under the raft. This feeling was much different.

I savored the moment with Debbie. I was totally smitten. Why was I falling for a girl who lived in another state?

"Honey, when you go back to Miami, will you write me?"

"Sure, sweetheart. I really want to keep in touch. After all, I am mascot of the drill team."

"I'll write you back. When you get a letter from me, make sure to smell it. It will remind you of our great day together," she cooed, as she leaned toward me and brushed her cheek against mine. I breathed in the lovely fragrance of her shampoo and cologne.

"Great. Send me a picture of you, too," I said, still slightly intoxicated by Debbie's kiss.

"I've got a cute picture of me in my drill team outfit. Will you show all your friends what your Texas girlfriend looks like?"

"Will I? Of course, Debbie. I wish you were a twirler in my high school's band. After football games, we could sit together in the back of the band bus."

"I'm really looking forward to next Christmas vacation in Miami. Grandma is just going to love you. When you come over to her apartment, I'll make sure she bakes something delicious for you. Her potato latkes are crispy and yummy. She serves them with sour cream and applesauce."

The carousel stopped, and we stepped down from it. "Come on, you two lovebirds, we need to get over to the travel agency and buy a ticket home for Rodya. Kenny, I'll see you Friday night. Pick me up at eight o'clock," said Marilyn. This time she gave her new boyfriend a long passionate kiss on the lips while stroking the back of his neck.

As we walked past the historic Cotton Bowl on the way back to the car, it was obvious Marilyn was very excited. "Kenny invited me to a dance at his parents' country club next week. I don't have a thing to wear. Suzy, you're the one with the great fashion sense. Let's plan a clothes shopping day so I can look my sexiest. I think I am falling in love with Kenny. Isn't he cute? ICB. I crave his bod."

✵ ✵ ✵

After a short drive through downtown Dallas, Marilyn parked the car several blocks from the travel agency. Walking through a seedy part of downtown Dallas made us all a little nervous. We sped up our pace after we noticed several guys leaning against the vacant buildings across the street. They looked menacing as they followed us with their eyes. There was danger lurking in the shadows of downtown Dallas. Finally we found it. The Lone Star Travel Agency.

I approached the ticket counter and loudly announced, "I need a one-way airplane ticket to Miami, Florida."

The ticket agent studied the schedule and responded, "If you don't mind making a few stops, I have a one-way ticket for only forty-four dollars. Leaving out of Love Field, you'll fly on a DC six. There will be stops in New Orleans and Birmingham, Alabama. Then you change planes in Atlanta. You'll fly on a jet to Miami, with stops in Jacksonville and Fort Lauderdale. The trip will take twelve hours, but at least it's faster than the Pony Express."

"That sounds okay with me. It's a lot quicker than taking the bus home. I'm sure Dad will be happy that I'm buying a ticket that's affordable. Of course, I am spending my own money."

As the agent drew up the ticket, a boy about my age walked away from his parents and came over to me.

"Pardon me, but I overheard you say you were going home to Miami. That's an ocean resort town, isn't it? I just love the Beach Boys and surfer music. Do you surf?" he asked in a thick British accent.

"Yeah, yeah, yeah, sure, I surf. Where are you from, London?"

"No, actually, I'm a Liverpudlian."

"Ha ha," laughed Suzy. "We just read *Gulliver's Travels* in English Lit. Are you a tiny person from Liverpudlia, where there are puddles of liver everywhere?"

"That's a good one. Let me explain. A Liverpudlian is a native of Liverpool, England. It's a city on the Mersey River. No surfing, I'm afraid."

"That's jolly interesting, old chap. Did the Texans give you any problems when you spoke with that British accent? They told me I talk like a Yankee," I informed him in my best Cockney accent.

"Yes, indeed. Quite right. It is apparent that these Rebels are still fighting you Yanks 100 years after your War Between the States. I'm afraid some of those Texas blokes got rather insulting about the way I speak. They seem to think it was America that saved England in World War II. I could have given them a history lesson but was worried that it might end in fisticuffs. I really prefer not getting shot by some bloody cowboy. I had trouble understanding their thick Texas drawls. You speak very clearly, though. I rather like your Miami accent."

"I love your British accent. It sounds so intelligent," said Suzy.

"If you like British accents and rock and roll music, then you'll love the new band that has been playing the clubs in Liverpool this year. They are the hardest rocking band ever. Great harmonies, and their antics on the stage are hilarious. Everyone in Liverpool is crazy about them. Especially the girls. They scream so loud it's hard to hear the music. I think they're going to be the hottest sound in pop music. You Americans are going to be singing rock and roll in British accents very soon."

"British rock and roll? I can't imagine. Rock and roll is as American as football, fried chicken, and the rodeo. American kids will never listen to pop music from England," I assured him.

"English boys playing rock and roll? Hey if it's rockin', I'm rockin'. I'm always ready to dance to a solid beat. Cute Liverpudlian guitar players? Jolly good, old chap. Hey, if you want to hear great sounds, listen to KBOX," said Marilyn, while gyrating her hips and doing the Twist.

"American rock and roll is great, but our day is coming. You'll see. It was jolly good meeting y'all. Cheerio."

As we walked out of the travel agency, I muttered under my breath in a slow Texas drawl, "British rock and roll? Ain't never gonna happen."

✵ ✵ ✵

It was getting dark as we walked back to the car. There were some panhandlers walking around asking for spare change. Newspapers and other litter blew around in the street. We stayed huddled in our tight group. Just as we were walking by, three Dallas policemen sauntered out of a nightclub. They were wearing white ten-gallon hats and nicely-pressed uniforms. There were guns visible in their shiny black holsters. When the door was opened, we could hear music coming from inside.

I opened the door, and Donny and I tried to peek inside. There was a strong smell of cigarette smoke and whiskey. I could see several men staring toward an elevated stage. Taking a few steps into the club, I could hear the familiar suggestive sound of the big hit record "The Stripper" being played. Donny and I craned our necks to see what was happening on that stage. A few more steps in, and there she was. A naked woman with sequined tassels covering her nipples had herself wrapped around a pole. The tiny thong panties she wore split her large round butt cheeks like dental floss. As I stepped forward, mesmerized, a very strong man in a fedora hat grabbed me roughly by the back of my shirt, almost lifting me off the ground.

"Not so fast, sonny. Yous children are not allowed in here. I don't want any trouble with law enforcement. If one of those Dallas cops saw you in my establishment they'd lock me up and throw away the key." Donny and I were quickly moved right back out the door.

"Rod, look at this," Donny pointed to the signs in the windows: "Nudity, Topless Girls, and Exotic Dancing All Night Long". A silhouette of a nude woman had been drawn on one of the signs that read "The Carousel Club".

I said to Donny, "Wow! A strip club, naked girls, and bare boobs. It must be great running a place like this. All the women you could ever imagine, all the time. The guy who runs this place must be the luckiest man in the world."

I glanced back at the marquee, which read "The Carousel Club. Proprietor, Jack Ruby".

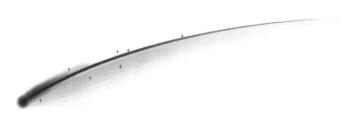

LOVE FIELD

"**I**T'S BEEN A wonderful vacation. Thanks for everything, Aunt Betty."

"Tell your Mom I'll be down for a Florida vacation next winter. I'm going to need a break from the cold. By Thanksgiving, that cold north wind starts blowing through Texas, and everyone gets a chill. This year I'm really dreading Dallas at Thanksgiving. Brrrrr," said Aunt Betty with a shudder, as if she had a premonition of some approaching disaster.

Uncle Will gave me a hug and said, "Roddy, it was great getting to know you this summer. I know Suzy and Marilyn enjoyed having you around. Do you remember meeting my cousin, Martha Mazurski? She just can't stop talking about how much you resemble her brother Rueven, who was murdered in the Holocaust. She told me she feels his spirit lives on in you. "When she came to Dallas after the war, she was a broken woman. She had seen so much of what she loved destroyed. Lately she's able to smile a little. Meeting you has been a great blessing for her."

"I love all my Texas cousins. You've been great to me. I'll never forget this summer in Texas. I'm going to miss everyone."

"Marilyn, drive safely. Suzy, help Roddy with his suitcase. Have a safe trip and give everyone in your family hugs and kisses from us," said Aunt Betty as she waved goodbye.

"I will, Mom. Rodya, you may sit shotgun one more time. Climb in to the old Galaxy. Suzy, backseat."

Marilyn backed out of the driveway and drove us down Timberview Drive. She changed channels on the radio until she came to a song she wanted to hear.

"Ooh, the Chiffons. This song reminds me of Kenny. Cause he's so fine," she said.

"When I came here, neither of you had boyfriends. Now you're both madly in love and have steady dates."

"Marilyn's the one who's in love. Donny's so nice, but I already told him I don't want to go steady now. I hated to hurt his feelings, but I couldn't accept the necklace he wanted me to wear. It was half of a golden heart. He wanted to wear the other half under his shirt. Maybe I'll reconsider in a few years when we get our braces off. Besides, Tommy Bello asked me out for next weekend. Tommy's kind of adorable. I wonder if he's a good kisser."

Marilyn interrupted, "Debbie Burns is one of the cutest girls on the drill team. I'm so jealous of those killer dimples. Rodya, you are a charmer. It's possible that she loves you."

"She loves me? Yeah, yeah, yeah. Debbie promised to keep in touch. She promised to write. Long-distance phone calls are way too expensive, and I wouldn't even think of asking Dad to let me call Debbie on our home phone. I'm so glad she's coming to Miami, Christmas vacation. Home is gonna be mighty dull after hanging out with y'all this summer."

"Listen to that Texas drawl. He said 'y'all'. Next thing you know he'll be saying 'yes ma'am' and 'no ma'am'," teased Marilyn.

"I'll be wearing my ten-gallon hat everywhere I go in Miami. Good thing you didn't buy me one of those stupid-looking Texas string ties."

"Here we are at the airport. Love Field. Texas has been a field of love for you, cuz. We'll walk you to the ticket counter."

Marilyn and Suzy walked into the airport with me. They each gave me a big hug.

"You two girls are like sisters to me, only better. We never fight. It's gonna be a blast when you come to Miami. You're going to get Coppertone tans."

"Bye, Roddy."

"Dasvidanya, Rodya."

"Adios, muchachas."

As they walked away, each blew me a kiss.

The line at the ticket counter was very short, especially considering my ambivalence about leaving. After a brief wait, the ticket agent greeted me.

"Are you traveling alone, young man?"

"Yes, ma'am."

"Do you have any luggage to check?"

"Yes, ma'am."

She leafed through my ticket. "Goodness, young man, look at all those stops. Don't lose your tickets or your luggage tag. Don't worry. Your bag will be transferred to your flight out of Atlanta. It's checked all the way to Miami. I'll make sure our flight attendants take good care of you. We try to treat every passenger leaving Love Field like they're the President of the United States. Have a wonderful trip. Gate 10 is to your left."

"Thank you, ma'am."

I sat down at the gate and watched the crew load the luggage under the plane. The stairway was rolled up to the door of the plane.

The announcement came from the gate agent: "Now boarding Flight 1615 to New Orleans, Birmingham, Alabama, and Atlanta, Georgia."

It was exciting climbing the stairs and boarding the DC-6. My seat was near the back. Lucky for me, the other two seats in my row were empty. I sat down and made myself comfortable. The stewardesses all wore cute uniforms with pillbox hats. One came over and made sure my seatbelt was fastened.

"How old are you, young man?"

"Thirteen, ma'am."

"If you need anything, just push the button on the overhead panel, and one of us will be there to help you. My name is Ellie. Relax and enjoy the flight."

As the airplane accelerated down the runway, I was pushed gently back in my seat. It was thrilling to watch the ground fall away as we gained elevation. I looked back at Love Field and the surrounding area. Bye, bye, Love. Bye, bye Big D. Hello, rest of my life. I feel like I can fly. I feel like I can fly.

After a few minutes of light turbulence, we passed through a layer of clouds. As we broke through the top layer, I looked out and gloried in the sight of blue skies above and billowy white cumulus clouds below. I was finally airborne.

The stewardesses started the food service. Ellie, wearing white gloves, put the meal on the tray in front of me. A complete dinner was served: roast beef, mash potatoes, and vegetables.

"Would you like coffee, tea, or milk, sir?"

"Coffee, with cream and sugar, please." Remembering Marilyn's risqué joke, I restrained myself from telling her that I liked my coffee just like I like my women.

"Enjoy your dinner, young man. I'll be around later with dessert. I hope you like peaches and cream."

"That's my favorite. Thank you, Ellie." I said, while admiring her lovely complexion and adorable dimple.

Eating dinner on the airplane felt like dining in a fine restaurant. I sat back to watch the sun set over the clouds. The colors in the sky grew very intense. Crimson red, burnt orange, golden yellow, and shades in between. As the top edge of the sun's disk dropped below the clouds, the colors merged, and I saw a flash of green. The memory of the shooting star burning across the Texas sky burned across my mind.

Feeling very relaxed and with a full stomach, I placed my seat in the fully reclined position. I pulled out the book *Stranger in a Strange Land*, which I'd bought at the Coral Gables bus terminal what seemed like ages ago. Opening the book and reading the first few pages, I realized I had been having so much fun during my weeks in Texas that I hadn't had a chance to read a single page. Stranger in a strange land. After my summer in Texas, I could relate.

Tired and unable to concentrate on reading, I reached up and pushed the button on the panel to turn off the overhead reading light. Bong! The call bell rang. Whoops, wrong button.

Two flight attendants came up to me immediately. "How can we help you?" asked Ellie.

"I'm sorry. I pushed the wrong button."

"Don't worry. It happens all the time. Monica, let's get this young man a pillow and a blanket."

Ellie lifted the armrests to the middle seat and aisle seat.

"You have a long night of flying ahead of you. Why don't you lie down across these three seats and try to get some sleep? Please keep your seatbelt loosely fastened."

Ellie handed me the pillow, and the tall slender Monica draped the blanket over me. She tucked me in and stroked my cheek like I was a child, but only for a second. Ellie reached up and turned off the call button.

With the pillow beneath my head, I thought back to my summer vacation. So many new experiences, so much fun with my cousins, so many new friends, and such lovely girls. Mary Beth ... Gayla ... I took a deep breath and closed my eyes. Peacefully, The refrain drifted through my thoughts, "*Two girls for every boy.*" Debbie ... Helen ...

Bong! "In preparation for landing, please place your seats in their upright positions. Make sure your seatbelt is securely fastened. We are on our final approach to Atlanta Municipal Airport."

Ellie and Monica walked down the aisle. Ellie stopped by my row and spoke with a thick Southern accent, "My, my, aren't you a sleepyhead. You slept through two landings and two take-offs. Monica and I decided to let you sleep since you looked so peaceful. You slept through the stops at New Orleans and Birmingham. You didn't even stir while we raised and lowered your seat. It's such a blessing that you are able to sleep while traveling on an airplane. So many passengers are nervous and are unable to rest while we're in the air. What a peaceful night you've had. Sweetie pie, you slept like a baby with a very clean conscience."

Thinking about the nearly 24 hours of staying awake on my trip west on the Greyhound, I laughed to myself, realizing I had been sleeping for nearly five hours. Airplanes: What a wonderful way to travel.

We taxied to a stop after landing in Atlanta. The engines exhaled a small amount of blue exhaust smoke as the propellers on the slowing DC-6 stopped rotating. The stairway was rolled to the plane and the door was opened. I followed the other passengers down the aisle and past the flight crew.

"Thank you for flying with us," said the pilot.

"Glad you had a restful flight. Goodnight, sugar," said Ellie.

Monica smiled sweetly, winked at me, and said, "Goodbye, hon."

I entered the airport and was greeted by a large sign that read "Welcome to Georgia, the Peach State". The sign was decorated by a large Georgia state flag that was nearly identical to the Confederate Stars and Bars. The Thomas Jefferson high school cheer, "Go Rebels", went through my mind.

I looked at the information board in the airport and found the gate and time for my flight to Miami. Because there was an hour and a half before boarding, I had time to explore the airport. There were posters on the concourse walls advertising points of interest located around Atlanta. "Climb Stone Mountain. See the largest piece of exposed granite in the world. Enjoy the giant sculpture on the southern Mount Rushmore. We honor three heroes of the Confederacy, Jefferson Davis, Stonewall Jackson, and Robert E. Lee all riding on horseback." The poster did not mention that Stone Mountain was the sight of the founding of the Ku Klux Klan. "Go Rebels".

Another poster had a drawing of Rhett Butler and Scarlet O'Hara: "Atlanta, home of Scarlet and Rhett. The Old South is not *Gone With the Wind*." "See Peachtree Street. Visit the historic Fox Theater", proclaimed another. Another poster was painted with colorful flowers: "The Dogwood Festival. Springtime in Atlanta. See the azalea, dogwood, and cherry trees in bloom."

I thought to myself, "Maybe someday I'll visit Atlanta and climb Stone Mountain. I'd love to get to know some more Southern girls. Atlanta girls must be peaches."

"Now Boarding Flight 1963. Jet to Miami, with intermediate stops in Jacksonville and Fort Lauderdale."

I boarded the Convair 880 jet by walking down the jetway, which connected the gate to the aircraft. The hum of the jet engines was louder but smoother than the sound the propellers had made on the DC-6.

The jet seemed to quiver with energy. Jet power. The acceleration down the runway was thrilling. The powerful surge of the jet engines pushed me back in my seat, as we seemed to jump off the runway and rapidly climb into the air. The lights of downtown Atlanta glowed brightly. A few streetlights were visible for a moment but faded from view as we rose above the clouds. A three-quarter moon shone brightly outside my window. The man in the moon seemed to smile at me. Was it a waxing moon or a waning moon?

The crossword puzzle in the airline magazine was an easy one. I almost had it solved when the seatbelt sign lit up with a bong, and we began our descent into Jacksonville. We landed and taxied to the gate. Most of the other passengers got off, but I stayed in my seat, watching the ground crew. I admired how they worked together efficiently as a team.

The flight to Fort Lauderdale was less than half full. I was nearly home. The powerful jet takeoff out of Jacksonville airport again thrilled me. The lights along the coast of Florida were visible, separating the land from the Atlantic Ocean. There were a few lights visible on the ocean. They must have been from boats traveling in the middle of the night. Some of the boats must be carrying people home from journeys to exotic ports.

Visiting Texas had been a blast. Someday I'll see the whole world.

We landed at Fort Lauderdale airport. This appeared to be the final destination for just about everyone.

The layover was very short. Looking around after the door was closed, I saw that there were only two or three other passengers on board for the short hop to Miami. The copilot walked through the cabin and stopped next to me.

"Looks like this flight is nearly empty. Young fella, would you like to sit up front in the jump seat? You'll be sitting in the cock pit behind me and the pilot."

"That would be amazing. I've been flying all night. Really? Sit up front with the crew?"

The copilot walked me to the front of the plane. The flight attendant pulled down the jump seat, which was located right behind the pilot's seat. Her name tag read Maria.

"It is somewhat unusual to allow a passenger to fly up here. We'll make an exception tonight, on this very short and nearly empty flight. I'm sure it will be fine," she said.

Seeing me struggle with the shoulder harness and seatbelt, Maria adjusted the length of the belt and secured me into a comfortable position.

"Thank you for assisting me, Maria. I really appreciate your help," I said, as the last buckle clicked closed.

The instrument panel was illuminated with an incredible number of bright lights, switches, and dials. I stayed quiet while the crew went through the preflight checklist with pre-cise attention to detail. Finally, we taxied to the runway and began accelerating for takeoff. The cockpit window seemed to surround me. The view was amazing. Visibility from the cockpit was so much better than looking out from a passenger window. The lights of the runway sped by faster and faster. The pilot pulled back on the wheel, and we gained altitude rapidly. The jet rose off the ground into the clear night sky of South Florida. The altimeter dial spun round and round like a fast moving clock.

"Are you headed home to Miami, young man?" the pilot asked me.

The landing gear retracted and locked with a thump.

"Yes, sir. I've just had a wonderful summer vacation in Texas," I said, marveling at glistening lights of South Florida that illumi-nated the city below me.

"Do you see that bright light there in the distance?" A rotating beacon was easily visible through the cockpit window.

"Yes, sir. I see it."

"That's the tower at Miami International Airport. Welcome home."

✳ ✳ ✳

ABOUT THE AUTHOR

Rodger Aidman is a native of Akron, Ohio, where he lived until he moved with his family to Miami, Florida, at age nine. He attended The Ohio State University and is a graduate of Emory University School of Dentistry. Dr. Aidman has practiced dentistry in South Miami since 1978. He lives in Pinecrest, Florida, with his wife Susan. Their daughter Ellyn lives in Tallahassee and is working on a doctorate in educational leadership. Their son Andrew is a talented song writer and musician and is currently enrolled in the Masters in Film program at the University of Southern California.

Summer of '63 is Dr. Aidman's first novel.

Made in the USA
Charleston, SC
01 November 2011